Races and Immigrants in America

Races and Immigrants in America

by John R. Commons

Copyright © 2/17/2016
Jefferson Publication

ISBN-13: 978-1530098750

Printed in the United States of America

All rights reserved. No part of this book may be reprinted or reproduced or utilized in any form or by any electronic, mechanical, or other means, now known or hereafter invented, including photocopying and recording, or in any form of storage or retrieval system, without prior permission in writing from the publisher.'

Table of Contents

CHAPTER I 3
    RACE AND DEMOCRACY 3
CHAPTER II 10
    COLONIAL RACE ELEMENTS 10
CHAPTER III 17
    THE NEGRO 17
CHAPTER IV 26
    NINETEENTH CENTURY ADDITIONS 26
CHAPTER V 43
    INDUSTRY 43
CHAPTER VI 56
    LABOR 56
CHAPTER VII 66
    CITY LIFE, CRIME, AND POVERTY 66
CHAPTER VIII 76
    POLITICS 76
CHAPTER IX 84
    AMALGAMATION AND ASSIMILATION 84

CHAPTER I

RACE AND DEMOCRACY

"All men are created equal." So wrote Thomas Jefferson, and so agreed with him the delegates from the American colonies. But we must not press them too closely nor insist on the literal interpretation of their words. They were not publishing a scientific treatise on human nature nor describing the physical, intellectual, and moral qualities of different races and different individuals, but they were bent upon a practical object in politics. They desired to sustain before the world the cause of independence by such appeals as they thought would have effect; and certainly the appeal to the sense of equal rights before God and the law is the most powerful that can be addressed to the masses of any people. This is the very essence of American democracy, that one man should have just as large opportunity as any other to make the most of himself, to come forward and achieve high standing in any calling to which he is inclined. To do this the bars of privilege have one by one been thrown down, the suffrage has been extended to every man, and public office has been opened to any one who can persuade his fellow-voters or their representatives to select him.

But there is another side to the successful operations of democracy. It is not enough that equal opportunity to participate in making and enforcing the laws should be vouchsafed to all—it is equally important that all should be capable of such participation. The individuals, or the classes, or the races, who through any mental or moral defect are unable to assert themselves beside other individuals, classes, or races, and to enforce their right to an equal voice in determining the laws and conditions which govern all, are just as much deprived of the privilege as though they were excluded by the constitution. In the case of individuals, when they sink below the level of joint participation, we recognize them as belonging to a defective or criminal or pauper class, and we provide for them, not on the basis of their rights, but on the basis of charity or punishment. Such classes are exceptions in point of numbers, and we do not feel that their non-participation is a flaw in the operations of democratic government. But when a social class or an entire race is unable to command that share in conducting government to which the laws entitle it, we recognize at once that democracy as a practical institution has in so far broken down, and that, under the forms of democracy, there has developed a class oligarchy or a race oligarchy.

Two things, therefore, are necessary for a democratic government such as that which the American people have set before themselves: equal opportunities before the law, and equal ability of classes and races to use those opportunities. If the first is lacking, we have legal oligarchy; if the second is lacking, we have actual oligarchy disguised as democracy.

Now it must be observed that, compared with the first two centuries of our nation's history, the present generation is somewhat shifting its ground regarding democracy. While it can never rightly be charged that our fathers overlooked the inequalities of races and individuals, yet more than the present generation did they regard with hopefulness the educational value of democracy. "True enough," they said, "the black man is not equal to the white man, but once free him from his legal bonds, open up the schools, the professions, the businesses, and the offices to those of his number who are most aspiring, and you will find that, as a race, he will advance favorably in comparison with his white fellow-citizens."

It is now nearly forty years since these opportunities and educational advantages were given to the negro, not only on equal terms, but actually on terms of preference over the whites, and the fearful collapse of the experiment is recognized even by its partisans as something that was inevitable in the nature of the race at that stage of its development. We shall have reason in the following pages to enter more fully into this discussion, because the race question in America has found its most intense expression in the relations between the white and the negro races, and has there shown itself to be the most fundamental of all American social and political problems. For it was this race question that precipitated the Civil War, with the ominous problems that have followed upon that catastrophe; and it is this same race problem that now diverts attention from the treatment of those pressing economic problems of taxation, corporations, trusts, and labor organizations which themselves originated in the Civil War. The race problem in the South is only one extreme of the same problem in the great cities of the North, where popular government, as our forefathers conceived it, has been displaced by one-man power, and where a profound distrust of democracy is taking hold upon the educated and property-holding classes who fashion public opinion.

This changing attitude toward the educational value of self-government has induced a more serious study of the nature of democratic institutions and of the classes and races which are called upon to share in them. As a people whose earlier hopes have been shocked by the hard blows of experience, we are beginning to pause and take invoice of the heterogeneous stocks of humanity that we have admitted to the management of our great political enterprise. We are trying to look beneath the surface and to inquire whether there are not factors of heredity and race more fundamental than those of education and environment. We find that our democratic theories and forms of government were fashioned by but one of the many races and peoples which have come within their practical operation, and that that race, the so-called Anglo-Saxon, developed them out of its own insular experience unhampered by inroads of alien stock. When once thus established in England and further developed in America we find that other races and peoples, accustomed to despotism and even savagery, and wholly unused to self-government, have been thrust into the delicate fabric. Like a practical people as we pride ourselves, we have begun actually to despotize our institutions in order to control these dissident elements, though still optimistically holding that we retain the original democracy. The earlier problem was mainly a political one—how to unite into one self-governing nation a scattered population with the wide diversity of natural resources, climates, and interests that mark a country soon to stretch from ocean to ocean and from the arctics to the subtropics. The problem now is a social one,—how to unite into one people a congeries of races even more diverse than the resources and climates from which they draw their subsistence. That motto, "*E pluribus unum*," which in the past has guided those who through constitutional debate and civil war worked out our form of government, must now again be the motto of those who would work out the more fundamental problem of divergent races. Here is something deeper than the form of government—it is the essence of government—for it is that union of the hearts and lives and abilities of the people which makes government what it really is.

The conditions necessary for democratic government are not merely the constitutions and laws which guarantee equality, liberty, and the pursuit of happiness, for these after all are but paper documents. They are not merely freedom from foreign power, for the Australian colonies enjoy the most democratic of all governments, largely because they are owned by another country which has protected them from foreign and civil wars. Neither are wealth and prosperity necessary for democracy, for these may tend to luxury, inequality, and envy. World power, however glorious and enticing, is not helpful to democracy, for it inclines to militarism and centralization, as did Rome in the hands of an emperor, or Venice in the hands of an oligarchy. The true foundations of democracy are in the character of the people themselves, that is, of the individuals who constitute the democracy. These are: first, intelligence—the power to weigh evidence and draw sound conclusions, based on adequate information; second, manliness, that which the Romans called virility, and which at bottom is dignified self-respect, self-control, and that self-assertion and jealousy of encroachment which marks those who, knowing their rights, dare maintain them; third, and equally important, the capacity for coöperation, that willingness and ability to organize, to trust their leaders, to work together for a common interest and toward a common destiny, a capacity which we variously designate as patriotism, public spirit, or self-government. These are the basic qualities which underlie democracy,—intelligence, manliness, coöperation. If they are lacking, democracy is futile. Here is the problem of races, the fundamental division of mankind. Race differences are established in the very blood and physical constitution. They are most difficult to eradicate, and they yield only to the slow processes of the centuries. Races may change their religions, their forms of government, their modes of industry, and their languages, but underneath all these changes they may continue the physical, mental, and moral capacities and incapacities which determine the real character of their religion, government, industry, and literature. Race and heredity furnish the raw material, education and environment furnish the tools, with which and by which social institutions are fashioned; and in a democracy race and heredity are the more decisive, because the very education and environment which fashion the oncoming generations are themselves controlled through universal suffrage by the races whom it is hoped to educate and elevate.

Social Classes.—Closely connected with race division in its effect upon democracy are the divisions between social classes. In America we are wont to congratulate ourselves on the absence of classes with their accompanying hatred and envy. Whether we shall continue thus to commend ourselves depends partly on what we mean by social classes. If we compare our situation with an extreme case, that of India, where social classes have been hardened into rigid castes, we can see the connection between races and classes. For it is generally held that the castes of India originated in the conquests by an Aryan race of an indigenous dark or colored race. And while the clear-cut race distinctions have been blended through many centuries of amalgamation, yet it is most apparent that a gradation in the color of the skin follows the gradation in social position, from the light-colored, high-caste Brahman to the dark-colored, low-caste Sudra, or outcast pariah. Race divisions have been forgotten, but in their place religion has sanctified a division even more rigid than that of race, for it is sacrilege and defiance of the gods when a man of low caste ventures into the occupation and calling of the high caste. India's condition now is what might be conceived for our Southern states a thousand years from now, when the black man who had not advanced to the lighter shades of mulatto should be excluded from all professions and skilled trades and from all public offices, and should be restricted to the coarsest kind of service as a day laborer or as a field hand on the agricultural plantations. Confined to this limited occupation, with no incentive to economize because of no prospect to rise above his station, and with his numbers increasing, competition would reduce his wages to the lowest limit consistent with the continuance of his kind. Such a development is plainly going on at the present day, and we may feel reasonably certain that we can see in our own South the very historical steps by which in the forgotten centuries India proceeded to her rigid system of castes.

There is lacking but one essential to the Indian system; namely, a religion which ascribes to God himself the inequalities contrived by man. For the Indian derives the sacred Brahman from the mouth of God, to be His spokesman on earth, while the poor Sudra comes from the feet of God, to be forever the servant of all the castes above him. But the Christian religion has set forth a different theory, which ascribes to God entire impartiality toward races and individuals. He has "made of one blood all nations." It is out of this doctrine that the so-called "self-evident" assertion in the Declaration of Independence originated, and it is this doctrine which throughout the history of European civilization has contributed to smoothen out the harsh lines of caste into the less definite lines of social classes. For it must be remembered that Europe, like India, is built upon conquest, and the earlier populations were reduced to the condition of slaves and serfs to the conquering races. True, there was not the extreme opposition of white and colored races which distinguished the conquests of India, and this is also one of the reasons why slavery and serfdom gradually gave way and races coalesced. Nevertheless, the peasantry of Europe to-day is in large part the product of serfdom and of that race-subjection which produced serfdom. Herein we may find the source of that arrogance on the one hand and subserviency on the other, which so closely relate class divisions to race divisions. The European peasant, says Professor Shaler, "knows himself to be by birthright a member of an inferior class, from which there is practically no chance of escaping.... It is characteristic of peasants that they have accepted this inferior lot. For generations they have regarded themselves as separated from their fellow-citizens of higher estate. They have no large sense of citizenly motives; they feel no sense of responsibility for any part of the public life save that which lies within their own narrow round of action."

How different from the qualities of the typical American citizen whose forefathers have erected our edifice of representative democracy! It was not the peasant class of Europe that sought these shores in order to found a free government. It was the middle class, the merchants and yeomen, those who in religion and politics were literally "protestants," and who possessed the intelligence, manliness, and public spirit which urged them to assert for themselves those inalienable rights which the church or the state of their time had arrogated to itself. With such a social class democracy is the only acceptable form of government. They demand and secure equal opportunities because they are able to rise to those opportunities. By their own inherent nature they look forward to and aspire to the highest positions.

But the peasants of Europe, especially of Southern and Eastern Europe, have been reduced to the qualities similar to those of an inferior race that favor despotism and oligarchy rather than democracy. Their only avenues of escape from their subordinate positions have been through the army and the church, and these two institutions have drawn from the peasants their ablest and brightest intellects into a life which deprived them of offspring. "Among the prosperous folk there have been ever many classes of occupations tempting the abler youths, while among the laborers the church has afforded the easiest way to rise, and that which is most tempting to the intelligent. The result has been, that while the priesthood and monastic orders have systematically debilitated all the populations of Catholic Europe, their influence has been most efficient in destroying talent in the peasant class."

Thus it is that the peasants of Catholic Europe, who constitute the bulk of our immigration of the past thirty years, have become almost a distinct race, drained of those superior qualities which are the foundation of democratic institutions. If in America our boasted freedom from the evils of social classes fails to be vindicated in the future, the reasons will be found in the immigration of races and classes incompetent to share in our democratic opportunities. Already in the case of the negro this division has hardened and seems destined to become more rigid. Therein we must admit at least one exception to our claim of immunity from social classes. Whether with our public schools, our stirring politics, our ubiquitous newspapers, our common language, and our network of transportation, the children of the European immigrant shall be able to rise to the opportunities unreached by his parents is the largest and deepest problem now pressing upon us. It behooves us as a people to enter into the practical study of this problem, for upon its outcome depends the fate of government of the people, for the people, and by the people.

Races in the United States.—We use the term "race" in a rather loose and elastic sense; and indeed we are not culpable in so doing, for the ethnographers are not agreed upon it. Races have been classified on the basis of color, on the basis of language, on the basis of supposed origin, and in these latter days on the basis of the shape of the skull. For our purpose we need consider only those large and apparent divisions which have a direct bearing on the problem of assimilation, referring those who seek the more subtle problems to other books.

Mankind in general has been divided into three and again into five great racial stocks, and one of these stocks, the Aryan or Indo-Germanic, is represented among us by ten or more subdivisions which we also term races. It need not cause confusion if we use the term "race" not only to designate these grand divisions which are so far removed by nature one from another as to render successful amalgamation an open question, but also to designate those peoples or nationalities which we recognize as distinct yet related within one of the large divisions. Within the area controlled by the United States are now to be found representatives of each of the grand divisions, or primary racial groups, and it would be a fascinating study to turn from the more practical topics before us and follow the races of man in their dispersion over the globe and their final gathering together again under the republic of America. First is the Aryan, or Indo-Germanic race, which, wherever it originated, sent its Sanskrit conquerors to the South to plant themselves upon a black race related to the Africans and the Australians. Its Western branch, many thousand miles away, made the conquest and settlement of Europe. Here it sent out many smaller branches, among them the Greeks and Latins, whose situation on the Mediterranean helped in great measure to develop brilliant and conquering civilizations, and who, after twenty centuries of decay and subjection, have within the past twenty years begun again their westward movement, this time to North and South America. North of Greece the Aryans became the manifold Slavs, that most prolific of races. One branch of the Slavs has spread the power of Russia east and west, and is now crushing the alien Hebrew, Finn, Lithuanian, and German, and even its fellow-Slav, the Pole, who, to escape their oppressors, are moving to America. The Russian himself, with his vast expanse of fertile prairie and steppe, does not migrate across the water, but drives away those whom he can not or will not assimilate. From Austria-Hungary, with its medley of races, come other branches of the Slavs, the Bohemians, Moravians, Slovaks, Slovenians, Croatians, Roumanians, Poles, and Ruthenians, some of them mistakenly called Huns, but really oppressed by the true Hun, the Magyar, and by the German. To the west of the Slavs we find the Teutonic branches of the Aryans, the Germans, the Scandinavians, and, above all, the English and Scotch-Irish with their descent from the Angles, Saxons, and Franks, who have given to America our largest accessions in numbers, besides our language, our institutions, and forms of government. Then other branches of the Aryans known as Celtic, including the Irish, Scotch, and Welsh, formerly driven into the hills and islands by the Teutons, have in these latter days vied with the English and Germans in adding to our population. The French, a mixture of Teuton and Celt, a nationality noted above all others for its stationary population and dislike of migration, are nevertheless contributing to our numbers by the circuitous route of Canada, and are sending to us a class of people more different from the present-day Frenchman in his native home than the Italian or Portuguese is different from the Frenchman.

In the fertile valleys of Mesopotamia and the Tigris the Semitic race had separated from its cousins, the Aryans, and one remarkable branch of this race, the Hebrews, settling on a diminutive tract of land on the eastern shore of the Mediterranean and finally driven forth as wanderers to live upon their wits, exploited by and exploiting in turn every race of Europe, have ultimately been driven forth to America by the thousands from Russia and Austria where nearly one-half of their present number is found.

Another race, the Mongolian, multiplying on the plains of Asia, sent a conquering branch to the west, scattering the Slavs and Teutons and making for itself a permanent wedge in the middle of Europe, whence, under the name of Magyar, the true Hungarian, the Mongolians come to America. Going in another direction from this Asiatic home the Mongolian race has made the circuit of the globe, and the Chinese, Japanese, and Koreans meet in America their unrecognized cousins of many thousand years ago.

Last of the immigrants to be mentioned, but among the earliest in point of time, is the black race from the slave coast of Africa. This was not a free and voluntary migration of a people seeking new fields to escape oppression, but a forced migration designed to relieve the white race of toil. All of the other races mentioned, the Aryan, the Semitic, the Mongolian, had in early times met one another and even perhaps had sprung from the same stock, so that when in America they come together there is presumably a renewal of former ties. But as far back as we can trace the history of races in the records of archæology or philology, we find no traces of affiliation with the black race. The separation by continents, by climate, by color, and by institutions is the most diametrical that mankind exhibits anywhere. It is even greater than that between the Aryan and the native American, improperly called the Indian, whose presence on the soil which we have seized from him has furnished us with a peculiar variation in our multiform race problem.

For the Indian tribes, although within our acquired territory, have been treated as foreign nations, and their reservations have been saved to them under the forms of treaties. Only recently has there sprung up a policy of admitting them to citizenship, and therefore the Indian, superior in some respects to the negro, has not interfered with our experiment in democracy.

Last in point of time we have taken into our fold the Malay race, with some seven million representatives in the Hawaiian and Philippine Islands. Like the Indian and the negro, this race never in historic times prior to the discovery of the new world came into close contact with the white races. With its addition we have completed the round of all the grand divisions of the human family, and have brought together for a common experiment in self-government the white, yellow, black, red, and brown races of the earth.

Amalgamation and Assimilation.—Scarcely another nation in ancient or modern history can show within compact borders so varied an aggregation. It is frequently maintained that a nation composed of a mixed stock is superior in mind and body to one of single and homogeneous stock. But it must be remembered that amalgamation requires centuries. The English race is probably as good an example of a mixed race as can be found in modern history, yet this race, though a mixture of the closely related primitive Celt, the conquering Teuton, and the Latinized Scandinavian, did not reach a common language and homogeneity until three hundred years after the last admixture. We know from modern researches that all of the races of Europe are mixed in their origin, but we also know that so much of that mixture as resulted in amalgamation occurred at a time so remote that it has been ascribed to the Stone Age. The later inroads have either been but temporary and have left but slight impression, or they have resulted in a division of territory. Thus the conquest of Britain by the Teutons and the Normans has not produced amalgamation so much as it has caused a segregation of the Celts in Scotland, Wales, and Ireland, and of the Teutons, with their later but slight infusion of Normans, in England. On the continent of Europe this segregation has been even more strongly marked. The present stratification of races and nationalities has followed the upheavals and inroads of a thousand years introduced by the decline and fall of the Roman Empire. Two developments have taken place. A conquering race has reduced a native population in part to subjection and has imposed upon the natives its laws, customs, and language. In course of time the subject race becomes a lower social class and slowly assimilates with the upper classes, producing a homogeneous nationality with a new evolution of laws, customs, and language. This is the history of four great nations of Europe,—the French, the German, the English, the Italian. The other development has been the segregation of a portion of the conquered race, who having fled their conquerors avoid actual subjection by escaping to the mountains and islands. Here they preserve their original purity of stock and language. This is the history of Austria-Hungary, whose earlier population of Slavs has been scattered right and left by German and Hun and who now constitute separate branches and dialects of the unassimilated races. That Austria-Hungary with its dozen languages should be able to hold together as a "dual empire" for many years is one of the marvels of history, and is frequently ascribed to that which is the essence of autocracy, the personal hold of the emperor.

The little bundle of republics known as Switzerland is a federation of French, Germans, and Italians, who retain their languages and have developed what out of such a conflict of races has elsewhere never been developed, a high grade of democratic government. Here in historic times there has been no amalgamation of races or assimilation of languages, but there has been the distinct advantage of a secluded freedom from surrounding feudal lords, which naturally led to a loose federation of independent cantons. It is Switzerland's mountains and not her mixed races that have promoted her democracy. At the other end of the world the highest development of democracy is in the colonies of Australasia, where a homogeneous race, protected from foreign foes, and prohibiting the immigration of alien races and inferior classes, has worked out self-government in politics and industry. In the Roman Empire we see the opposite extreme. At first a limited republic, the extension of conquests, and the incorporation of alien races led to that centralization of power in the hands of one man which transformed the republic into the empire. The British Empire, which to-day covers all races of the earth, is growingly democratic as regards Englishmen, but despotic as regards subject races. Taking the empire as a whole, neither amalgamation nor self-government is within the possibilities of its constitutional growth.

In America, on the other hand, we have attempted to unite all races in one commonwealth and one elective government. We have, indeed, a most notable advantage compared with other countries where race divisions have undermined democracy. A single language became dominant from the time of the earliest permanent settlement, and all subsequent races and languages must adopt the established medium. This is essential, for it is not physical amalgamation that unites mankind; it is mental community. To be great a nation need not be of one blood, it must be of one mind. Racial inequality and inferiority are fundamental only to the extent that they prevent mental and moral assimilation. If we think together, we can act together, and the organ of common thought and action is common language. Through the prism of this noble instrument of the human mind all other instruments focus their powers of assimilation upon the new generations as they come forth from the disunited immigrants. The public schools, the newspapers, the books, the political parties, the trade unions, the religious propagandists with their manifold agencies of universal education, the railroads with their inducements to our unparalleled mobility of population, are all dependent upon our common language for their high efficiency. Herein are we fortunate in our plans for the Americanization of all races within our borders. We are not content to let the fate of our institutions wait upon the slow and doubtful processes of blood amalgamation, but are eager to direct our energies toward the more rapid movements of mental assimilation. Race and heredity may be beyond our organized control; but the instrument of a common language is at hand for conscious improvement through education and social environment.

CHAPTER II

COLONIAL RACE ELEMENTS

Doubtless the most fascinating topic in the study of races is that of the great men whom each race has produced. The personal interest surrounding those who have gained eminence carries us back over each step of their careers to their childhood, their parents, and their ancestry. Pride of race adds its zest, and each race has its eulogists who claim every great man whose family tree reveals even a single ancestor, male or female, near or remote, of the eulogized race. Here is a "conflict of jurisdiction," and the student who is without race prejudice begins to look for causes other than race origin to which should be ascribed the emergence of greatness.

Mr. Henry Cabot Lodge attempted, some years ago, to assign to the different races in America the 14,243 men eminent enough to find a place in "Appleton's Encyclopedia of American Biography." He prepared a statistical summary as follows:—

EMINENT AMERICANS

English	10,376
Scotch-Irish	1,439
German	659
Huguenot	589
Scotch	436
Dutch	336
Welsh	159
Irish	109
French	85
Scandinavian	31
Spanish	7
Italian	7
Swiss	5
Greek	3
Russian	1
Polish	1
Total	14,243

When we inquire into the methods necessarily adopted in preparing a statistical table of this kind we discover serious limitations. Mr. Lodge was confined to the paternal line alone, but if, as some biologists assert, the female is the conservative element which holds to the type, and the male is the variable element which departs from the type, then the specific contribution of the race factor would be found in the maternal line. However, let this dubious point pass. We find that in American life two hundred years of intermingling has in many if not in most cases of greatness broken into the continuity of race. True, the New England and Virginia stock has remained during most of this time of purely English origin, but the very fact that in Mr. Lodge's tables Massachusetts has produced 2686 notables, while Virginia, of the same blood, has produced only 1038, must lead to the suspicion that factors other than race extraction are the mainspring of greatness.

It must be remembered that ability is not identical with eminence. Ability is the product of ancestry and training. Eminence is an accident of social conditions. The English race was the main contributor to population during the seventeenth century, and English conquest determined the form of government, the language, and the opportunities for individual advancement. During the succeeding century the Scotch-Irish and the Germans migrated in nearly equal numbers, and their combined migration was perhaps as great as that of the English in the seventeenth century. But they were compelled to move to the interior, to become frontiersmen, to earn their living directly from the soil, and to leave to their English-sprung predecessors the more prominent occupations of politics, literature, law, commerce, and the army. The Germans, who, according to Lodge, "produced fewer men of ability than any other race in the United States," were further handicapped by their language and isolation, which continue to this day in the counties of Pennsylvania where they originally settled. On the other hand, the Huguenots and the Dutch came in the first century of colonization. They rapidly merged with the English, lost their language, and hence contributed their full share of eminence. Finally, the Irish, Scandinavian and other races, inconspicuous in the galaxy of notables, did not migrate in numbers until the middle of the nineteenth century, and, in addition to the restraints of language and poverty, they found the roads to prominence preoccupied.

"Return of the Mayflower"
Painting by Boughton, 1834

Besides the accident of precedence in time, a second factor distinct from race itself has contributed to the eminence of one race over another. The Huguenots and the French, according to Lodge's statistics, show a percentage of ability in proportion to their total immigration much higher than that of any other race. But the Huguenots were a select class of people, manufacturers and merchants, perhaps the most intelligent and enterprising of Frenchmen in the seventeenth century. Furthermore the direct migration from France to this country has never included many peasants and wage-earners, but has been limited to the adventurous and educated. Had the French-Canadians who represent the peasantry of France been included in these comparisons, the proportion of French eminence would have been materially reduced.

The same is true of the English. Although sprung from one race, those who came to America represented at least two grades of society as widely apart as two races. The Pilgrims and Puritans of New England were the yeomen, the merchants, the manufacturers, skilled in industry, often independent in resources, and well trained in the intellectual controversies of religion and politics. The Southern planters also sprang from a class of similar standing, though not so strongly addicted to intellectual pursuits. Beneath both these classes were the indentured servants, a few of whom were men of ability forced to pay their passage by service. But the majority of them were brought to this country through the advertisements of shipowners and landholders or even forcibly captured on the streets of cities or transported for crimes and pauperism. Though all of these classes were of the same race, they were about as widely divergent as races themselves in point of native ability and preparatory training.

The third and most important cause of eminence, apart from ancestry, is the industrial and legal environment. An agricultural community produces very few eminent men compared with the number produced where manufactures and commerce vie with agriculture to attract the youth. A state of widely diversified industrial interests is likely to create widely diversified intellectual and moral interests. Complicated problems of industry and politics stimulate the mind and reflect their influence in literature, art, education, science, and the learned professions. Most of all, equal opportunity for all classes and large prizes for the ambitious and industrious serve to stimulate individuals of native ability to their highest endeavor. It was the deadening effects of slavery, creating inequalities among the whites themselves, that smothered the genius of the Southerner whether Englishman, Huguenot, or Scotch-Irish, and it was the free institutions of the North that invited their genius to unfold and blossom.

These considerations lead us to look with distrust on the claims of those who find in race ancestry or in race intermixture the reasons for such eminence as Americans have attained. While the race factor is decisive when it marks off inferior and primitive races, yet, in considering those Europeans races which have joined in our civilization, the important questions are: From what social classes is immigration drawn? and, Do our social institutions offer free opportunity and high incentive to the youth of ability? In so far as we get a choice selection of immigrants, and in so far as we afford them free scope for their native gifts, so far do they render to our country the services of genius, talent, and industry.

Incentives to Immigration.—It is the distinctive fact regarding colonial migration that it was Teutonic in blood and Protestant in religion. The English, Dutch, Swedes, Germans, and even the Scotch-Irish, who constituted practically the entire migration, were less than two thousand years ago one Germanic race in the forests surrounding the North Sea. The Protestant Reformation, sixteen centuries later, began among those peoples and found in them its sturdiest supporters. The doctrines of the Reformation, adapted as they were to the strong individualism of the Germanic races, prepared the hearts of men for the doctrines of political liberty and constitutional government of the succeeding century. The Reformation banished the idea that men must seek salvation through the intercession of priests and popes, who, however sacred, are only fellow-men, and set up the idea that each soul has direct access to God. With the Bible as a guide and his own conscience as a judge, each man was accountable only to one divine sovereign.

From the standpoint of the age this doctrine was too radical. It tended to break up existing society into sects and factions, and to precipitate those civil and religious wars which ended in a Catholic or aristocratic reaction. When this reaction came, the numerous Protestant sects of the extremer types found themselves the objects of persecution, and nothing remained but to seek a new land where the heavy hand of repression could not reach them. Thus America became the home of numberless religious sects and denominations of these several races. From England came Congregationalists (the "Pilgrims"), Puritans, Quakers, Baptists; from Scotland and Ireland came Presbyterians; from Germany came Quakers, Dunkards, Pietists, Ridge Hermits, Salzburgers, and Moravians.

It is not to be inferred that religious persecution alone in the early colonial period caused emigration. In point of numbers commercial enterprise was probably equally influential. In Holland all religious sects were welcomed with a liberality far in advance of any other nation, and at the same time the Dutch people were the most advanced in the modern pursuits of trade and commerce. The Dutch settlement of New Amsterdam was therefore a business enterprise, and neither before nor after the conquest by the British was there any religious obstacle to the reception of other races and religions. In this respect New York differed widely from New England, where religious exclusiveness preserved the English race as a peculiar people until the middle of the nineteenth century. So diverse were the races in New York, and so liberal were the opportunities open to all, that Governor Horatio Seymour was able to say that nine men prominent in its early history represented the same number of nationalities. Schuyler was of Dutch descent, Herkimer of German, Jay of French, Livingston of Scotch, Clinton of Irish, Morris of Welsh, Hoffman of Swedish, while Hamilton was a West India Englishman and Baron Steuben a Prussian.

Another colony to which all races and religions were welcomed was Pennsylvania. William Penn established this colony both as a refuge for the persecuted Quakers of England and as a real estate venture. He was the first American to advertise his dominions widely throughout Europe, offering to sell one hundred acres of land at two English pounds and a low rental. His advertisements combined humanity and business, for they called attention to popular government and universal suffrage; equal rights to all regardless of race or religious belief; trial by jury; murder and treason the only capital crimes, and reformation, not retaliation, the object of punishment for other offences. Thus Pennsylvania, although settled a half century later than the Southern and Northern colonies, soon exceeded them in population. Penn sent his agents to Germany and persuaded large numbers of German Quakers and Pietists to cast their lot in his plantation, so that in twenty years the Germans numbered nearly one-half the population. Again, in the beginning of the eighteenth century, when Louis XIV overran the Palatinate and thousands of Germans fled to England, the English government encouraged their migration to America. In one year four thousand of them, the largest single emigration of the colonial period, embarked for New York, but their treatment was so illiberal that they moved to Pennsylvania, and thenceforth the German migration sought the latter colony. These people settled at Germantown, near Philadelphia, and occupied the counties of Bucks and Montgomery, where they continue to this day with their peculiar language, the "Pennsylvania Dutch." Not only William Penn himself, but other landowners in Pennsylvania and also the shipowners advertised the country in Germany, and thousands of the poorer sort of Germans were induced to indenture themselves to the settlers to whom they were auctioned off by the ship captains in payment for transportation. Probably one-half of all the immigrants of the colonial period came under this system of postpaid transportation, just as at the present time nearly two-thirds come on prepaid tickets. It was in Pennsylvania that the largest portion of the Scotch-Irish settled, and before the time of the Revolution that colony had become the most populous and most diversified of all the colonies. It was the only colony, except Maryland, that tolerated Roman Catholics, and with all phases of the Christian religion and all branches of the Teutonic and Celtic races, Pennsylvania set the original type to which all of America has conformed, that of race intermixture on the basis of religious and political equality.

The Scotch-Irish.—It has long been recognized that among the most virile and aggressive people who came to America in colonial times, and who have contributed a peculiar share to the American character, are the Scotch-Irish. Their descendants boast of their ancestry and cite long lists of notables as their coderivatives. Yet until recent years it has been the misfortune of the Scotch-Irish to have escaped historical investigation; for American history has been written chiefly in New England, whose colonial Puritans forbade them in their midst. In fact, from the earliest settlement, the Scotch-Irish have been pioneers and men of action. They have contributed to America few writers and artists, but many generals, politicians, and captains of industry. In literature they claim two eminent names, Irving and Poe; but in the army, navy, politics, and business they claim John Paul Jones, Perry, Andrew Jackson, Winfield Scott, Zachary Taylor, Ulysses S. Grant, Stonewall Jackson, George B. McClellan, Alexander Hamilton, John C. Calhoun, James G. Blaine, Jefferson Davis, Thomas Benton, Hendricks, John G. Carlisle,

Mark Hanna, William McKinley, Matthew S. Quay, Andrew Carnegie, John D. Rockefeller, Horace Greeley, Henry Watterson, and hundreds alike famous in the more strenuous movements of American life.

A paradoxical fact regarding the Scotch-Irish is that they are very little Scotch and much less Irish. That is to say, they do not belong mainly to the so-called Celtic race, but they are the most composite of all the people of the British Isles. They are called Scots because they lived in Scotia, and they are called Irish because they moved to Ireland. Geography and not ethnology has given them their name. They are a mixed race through whose veins run the Celtic blood of the primitive Scot and Pict, the primitive Briton, the primitive Irish, but with a larger admixture of the later Norwegian, Dane, Saxon, and Angle. How this amalgamation came about we may learn from the geography of Scotland.

The Highlands of Scotland begin at the Grampian Hills and the Lowlands extend south from this line to the British border, and include the cities of Glasgow and Edinburgh. The Scotch-Irish came from that southwestern part of the Lowlands which bulges out toward Ireland north of the Solway Firth. Over these Lowland counties, bounded by water and hills on three sides, successive waves of conquest and migration followed. First the primitive Caledonian or Pict was driven to the Highlands, which to this day is the Celtic portion of Scotland. The Briton from the south, pressed on by Roman and then by Teuton, occupied the country. Then Irish tribes crossed over and gained a permanent hold. Then the Norwegian sailors came around from the north, and to this day there are pure Scandinavian types on the adjacent islands. Then the Saxons and Angles, driven by the Danes and Normans, gained a foothold from the east, and lastly the Danes themselves added their contingent. Here in this Lowland pocket of territory, no larger than a good-sized American county, was compounded for five hundred years this remarkable amalgam of races.

A thousand years later, after they had become a united people and had shown their metal in the trying times of the Reformation, they furnished the emigrants who displaced the Irish in the north of Ireland. James I, whom Scotland gave to England, determined to transform Catholic Ireland into Protestant England, and thereupon confiscated the lands of the native chiefs in Ulster and bestowed them upon Scottish and English lords on condition that they settle the territory with tenants from Scotland and England. This was the "great settlement" of 1610, and from that time to the present Ulster has been the Protestant stronghold of Ireland. In 1901 the population of Ulster was 44 per cent Catholic, 23 per cent Episcopalian, and 27 per cent Presbyterian, an ecclesiastical division corresponding almost exactly to the racial division of Irish, English, and Scotch. During the whole of the seventeenth century—the first century of this occupation—the Catholics and Episcopalians were in a much smaller proportion than these figures show for the present time, and the relative increase in Irish and Episcopalians during the eighteenth century was closely connected with the migration of the Scotch to America.

For one hundred years the Scotch multiplied in Ulster and had no dealings with the remnants of the Irish, whom they crowded into the barren hills and whom they treated like savages. They retained their purity of race, and although when they came to America they called themselves Irish and were known as Irish wherever they settled, yet they had no Irish blood except that which entered into their composition through the Irish migration to Scotia fifteen hundred years before.

Yet, though they despised the Irish, they could not escape the unhappy fate of Ireland. The first blow came in 1698, nearly one hundred years after their settlement. English manufacturers complained of Irish competition, and the Irish Parliament, a tool of the British crown, passed an act totally forbidding the exportation of Irish woollens, and another act forbidding the exportation of Irish wool to any country save England. Their slowly growing linen industry was likewise discriminated against in later years. Presbyterian Ulster had been the industrial centre of Ireland, and these acts nearly destroyed her industry. Next Queen Anne's Parliament adopted penal laws directed against Roman Catholics and Presbyterians, and the Test Act, which compelled public officials to take the communion of the Established Church, deprived the entire Scotch population of self-government. Nevertheless they were compelled to pay tithes to support the Established Church to which they were opposed. Lastly, the hundred-year leases of the tenants began to run out, and the landlords offered renewals to the highest bidders on short leases. Here the poverty-stricken Irish gained an unhappy revenge on the Scotch who had displaced them of their ancestral lands, for their low standard of living enabled them to offer rack-rents far above what the Scotch could afford. No longer did religion, race pride, or gratitude have a part in holding Ulster to Protestant supremacy. The greed of absentee landlords began to have full sway, and in the resulting struggle for livelihood, hopeless poverty was fitter to survive than ambitious thrift.

The Scotch tenants, their hearts bitter against England and aristocracy, now sought a country where they might have free land and self-government. In 1718 it is stated that 4200 of them left for America. After the famine of 1740 there were 12,000 who left annually. Altogether, in the half century just preceding the American Revolution, 200,000 persons, or one-third of the Protestant population of Ulster, are said to have emigrated, and the majority came to America. This was by far the largest contribution of any race to the population of America during the eighteenth century, and the injustice they suffered at the hands of England made them among the most determined and effective recruits to the armies that won our independence.

Before the Scotch-Irish moved to America the Atlantic coast line had been well occupied. Consequently, in order to obtain land for themselves, they were forced to go to the interior and to become frontiersmen. They found in Massachusetts a state church to which they must conform in order to be admitted to citizenship. But what they had left Ireland to escape they would not consent in a new country to do. The Puritans were willing that they should occupy the frontier as a buffer against the Indians, and so they took up lands in New Hampshire, Vermont, Western Massachusetts, and Maine. Only a few congregations, however, settled in New England—the bulk of the immigrants entered by way of Philadelphia and Baltimore and went to the interior of Pennsylvania surrounding and south of Harrisburg. They spread through the Shenandoah valley and in the foothill regions of Virginia and North and South Carolina. Gradually, they pushed farther west, across the mountains into Western Pennsylvania about Pittsburg, and into Ohio, Kentucky, and Tennessee. In all of these regions they fought the Indians, protected the older inhabitants from inroads, and developed those pioneer qualities which for one hundred years have characterized the "winning of the West."

Anglo-Saxon Mountaineers, Berea College, Kentucky

The Scotch-Irish occupied a peculiar place in the new world. More than any other race they served as the amalgam to produce, out of divergent races, a new race, the American. The Puritans of New England, the Quakers of Pennsylvania, the Cavaliers of Virginia, were as radically different as peoples of different races, and they were separated from each other in their own exclusive communities. The Germans were localized in Pennsylvania and Maryland, the Dutch in New York, but the Scotch-Irish "alone of the various races in America were present in sufficient numbers in all of the colonies to make their influence count; and they alone of all the races had one uniform religion; had experienced together the persecutions by state and church which had deprived them at home of their civil and religious liberties; and were the common heirs to those principles of freedom and democracy which had been developed in Scotland as nowhere else. At the time of the American Revolution there were ... in all above five hundred settlements scattered over practically all the American colonies." Trained as they were in the representative democracy of the Scottish kirk, thrown on their own resources in the wilderness, mingling with the pioneers of many other races, they took the lead in developing that Western type which in politics and industry became ultimately the American type; yet they retained their original character, and the American to-day is more at home in Glasgow than in London.

CHAPTER III

THE NEGRO

Although the negro races of Africa extend across the continent and from the Sudan to Cape Colony, yet the races which yielded the largest supply of slaves for America were confined to a narrow stretch of the Atlantic coast near the equator. For nearly two thousand miles from Cape Verde the coast of Africa runs southeast and easterly, and then for another thousand miles it runs to the south, forming the Gulf of Guinea, and from a belt of land along this coast practically all the negro immigrants to America have come. Here several large rivers, the Senegal, the Gambia, the Niger, and the Congo—furnished harbors for slave ships and routes for slave traders from the interior. Two circumstances, the climate and the luxuriant vegetation, render this region hostile to continuous exertion. The torrid heat and the excessive humidity weaken the will and exterminate those who are too strenuous; but this same heat and humidity, with the fertile soil, produce unparalleled crops of bananas, yams, and grains. Thus nature conspires to produce a race indolent, improvident, and contented. Seventy-five per cent of the deaths are said to be executions for supposed witchcraft, which has killed more men and women than the slave trade. Formerly cannibalism prevailed, but it has now been largely stamped out by European governments. The native governments are tribal, and the chiefs sustain themselves by their physical prowess and the help of priests and medicine men. Property is mainly in women and slaves, and inheritance is through the female, except among the nobility of Dahomey, where primogeniture rules. Written laws and records are unknown. The people are unstable, indifferent to suffering, and "easily aroused to ferocity by the sight of blood or under great fear." They exhibit aversion to silence and solitude, love of rhythm, excitability, and lack of reserve. All travellers speak of their impulsiveness, strong sexual passion, and lack of will power.

    Such, in brief, were the land and the people that furnished one-sixth of our total population and two-fifths of our Southern population. In shifting such a people from the torrid climate of equatorial Africa to the temperate regions of America, and from an environment of savagery to one of civilization, changes more momentous than those of any other migration have occurred. First, it was only the strongest physical specimens who survived the horrible tests of the slave catcher and the slave ship. Slavery, too, as a system, could use to best advantage those who were docile and hardy, and not those who were independent and feeble. Just as in the many thousand years of man's domestication of animals, the breechy cow and the balky horse have been almost eliminated by artificial selection, so slavery tended to transform the savage by eliminating those who were self-willed, ambitious, and possessed of individual initiative. Other races of immigrants, by contact with our institutions, have been civilized—the negro has been only domesticated. Democratic civilization offers an outlet for those who are morally and intellectually vigorous enough to break away from the stolid mass of their fellows; domestication dreads and suppresses them as dangerous rebels. The very qualities of intelligence and manliness which are essential for citizenship in a democracy were systematically expunged from the negro race through two hundred years of slavery. And then, by the cataclysm of a war in which it took no part, this race, after many thousand years of savagery and two centuries of slavery, was suddenly let loose into the liberty of citizenship and the electoral suffrage. The world never before had seen such a triumph of dogmatism and partizanship. It was dogmatism, because a theory of abstract equality and inalienable rights of man took the place of education and the slow evolution of moral character. It was partisanship, because a political party, taking advantage of its triumph in civil war, sought to perpetuate itself through the votes of its helpless beneficiaries. No wonder that this fateful alliance of doctrinaires and partizans brought fateful results, and that, after a generation of anarchy and race hatred, the more fundamental task of education has only just begun.

    True, there was a secondary object in view in granting the freedmen suffrage. The thirteenth amendment, adopted in 1865, legalized and extended the proclamation of emancipation, which had been a war measure. But this was followed by servile and penal laws in all the Southern states that looked like peonage in place of slavery. Congress then submitted the fourteenth amendment, which was adopted in 1867, creating a new grade of citizenship—citizenship of the nation—and prohibiting any state from depriving "any person of life, liberty, or property without the due process of law" and from denying to any person "the equal protection of the laws." But this was not enough. The next step was the fifteenth amendment adopted in 1869, prohibiting any state from denying the suffrage to citizens of the United States "on account of race, color, or previous condition of servitude." Thus equality before the law was to be protected by equality in making the law. This object was a worthy one, and it added the appearance of logical necessity to the theories of doctrinaires and the schemes of partisans. But it failed because based on a wrong theory of the ballot. Suffrage means self-government. Self-government means intelligence, self-control, and capacity for coöperation. If these are lacking, the ballot only makes way for the "boss," the corruptionist, or the oligarchy. The suffrage must be earned, not merely conferred, if it is to be an instrument of self-protection.

But it is the peculiar fate of race problems that they carry contestants to bitter extremes and afford no field for constructive compromise. Could the nation have adopted Lincoln's project of a hundred years, or even thirty years, of gradual emancipation, it might have avoided both the evils of war and the fallacies of self-government. But the spirit of race aggrandisement that precipitated the one rendered the other inevitable. With the negro suddenly made free by conquest, each fatal step in reconstruction was forced by the one that preceded. The North, the South, and the negro were placed in an impossible situation, and a nation which dreaded negro suffrage in 1868 adopted it in 1869.

For eight years the government of the Southern states was in the hands of the negroes. The result of turning the states over to ignorant and untried voters was an enormous increase of debt without corresponding public improvements or public enterprises. Even the negro governments themselves began to repudiate these debts and they were almost wholly repudiated by the whites after returning to power.

It is not necessary to dwell upon the methods by which the white voters regained and kept control of the states. Admittedly it was through intimidation, murder, ballot-box "stuffing," and false counting. The negro vote has almost disappeared, and in more recent years that which was accomplished through violence is perpetuated through law. Mississippi, Louisiana, South Carolina, North Carolina, Alabama, and Virginia have adopted so-called "educational" tests with such adroit exceptions that white illiterates may vote, but negroes, whether literate or illiterate, may be excluded from voting. As stated by a prominent white Virginian, "the negro can vote if he has $300, or if he is a veteran of the Federal or Confederate armies, or if he is a profound constitutional lawyer." The fifteenth amendment, by decisions of the United States Supreme Court, has been rendered inoperative, and the fourteenth amendment, without helping the negro, for whom it was designed, has raised up government by private corporations which never had been thought of as needing an amendment. With these decisions it may be taken for granted that the negro will not again in the near future enjoy the privilege of a free ballot.

This is a situation in which the North is as deeply interested as the South. The South, during the period of slavery, through the privilege of counting three-fifths of the slaves, enjoyed a predominance in Congress and in presidential elections beyond its proportion of white voters. The South now enjoys a greater privilege because it counts all the negroes. The fourteenth amendment expressly provides for a situation like this. It says:—

"When the right to vote at any election for the choice of electors for president and vice-president of the United States, representatives in Congress, the executive and judicial officers of a state, or the members of the legislature thereof, is denied to any of the male inhabitants of such state, being twenty-one years of age and citizens of the United States, or in any way abridged, except for participation in rebellion or other crime, the basis of representation shall be reduced in the proportion which the number of such male citizens shall bear to the whole number of male citizens twenty-one years of age in such state."

Whether it will be possible under our form of government to carry out this provision of the fourteenth amendment may be doubted, but that it is fast becoming a question of live interest is certain. The educational test is a rational test, but it is rational only when the state makes an honest and diligent effort to equip every man to pass the test. The former slave states spend $2.21 per child for educating the negroes, and $4.92 per child for educating the whites. The great lesson already learned is that we must "begin over again" the preparation of the negro for citizenship. This time the work will begin at the bottom by educating the negro for the ballot, instead of beginning at the top by giving him the ballot before he knows what it should do for him. What shall be the nature of this education?

Education and Self-help.—We have argued that democracy must be based upon intelligence, manliness, and coöperation. How can these qualities be produced in a race just emerged from slavery?

Intelligence is more than books and letters—it is knowledge of the forces of nature and ingenuity enough to use them for human service. The negro is generally acknowledged to be lacking in "the mechanical idea." In Africa he hardly knows the simplest mechanical principles. In America the brightest of the negroes were trained during slavery by their masters in the handicrafts, such as carpentry, shoemaking, spinning, weaving, blacksmithing, tailoring, and so on. A plantation became a self-supporting unit under the oversight and discipline of the whites. But the work of the negro artisans was careless and inefficient. The negro blacksmith fastened shoes to the plantation mule, but the horses were taken to the white blacksmith in town. Since emancipation the young generation has not learned the mechanical trades to the same extent as the slave generations. Moreover, as machinery supplants tools and factories supplant handicrafts, the negro is left still farther behind. "White men," says a negro speaker, "are bringing science and art into menial occupations and lifting them beyond our reach. In my boyhood the walls and ceilings were whitewashed each spring by colored men; now this is done by a white man managing a steam carpet-cleaning works. Then the laundry work was done by negroes; now they are with difficulty able to manage the new labor-saving machinery." Even in the non-mechanical occupations the negro is losing where he once had a monopoly. In Chicago "there is now scarcely a negro barber in the business district. Nearly all the janitor work in the large buildings has been taken away from them by the Swedes. White men and women as waiters have supplanted colored men in nearly all the first-class hotels and restaurants. Practically all of the shoe polishing is now done by Greeks."

Individual negroes have made great progress, but what we need to know is whether the masses of the negroes have advanced. The investigators of Atlanta University, in summarizing the reports of three hundred and forty-four employers of negroes, conclude: "There are a large number of negro mechanics all over the land, but especially in the South. Some of these are progressive, efficient workmen. More are careless, slovenly, and ill-trained. There are signs of lethargy among these artisans, and work is slipping from them in some places; in others they are awakening and seizing the opportunities of the new industrial South."

The prejudice of white workmen has undoubtedly played a part in excluding the negro from mechanical trades, but the testimony of large employers, who have no race prejudice where profits can be made, also shows that low-priced negro labor often costs more than high-priced white labor. The iron and steel mills of Alabama have no advantage in labor cost over mills of Pennsylvania and Ohio.

The foundation of intelligence for the modern workingman is his understanding of mechanics. Not until he learns through manual and technical training to handle the forces of nature can the workingman rise to positions of responsibility and independence. This is as important in agricultural labor, to which the negro is largely restricted, as in manufactures. Intelligence in mechanics leads to intelligence in economics and politics, and the higher wages of mechanical intelligence furnish the resources by which the workman can demand and secure his political and economic rights.

The second requisite of democracy is independence and manliness. These are moral qualities based on will power and steadfastness in pursuit of a worthy object. But these qualities are not produced merely by exhortation and religious revivals. They have a more prosaic and secular foundation. History shows that no class or nation has risen to independence without first accumulating property. However much we disparage the qualities of greed and selfishness which the rush for wealth has made obnoxious, we must acknowledge that the solid basis of the virtues is thrift. The improvidence of the negro is notorious. His neglect of his horse, his mule, his machinery, his eagerness to spend his earnings on finery, his reckless purchase of watermelons, chickens, and garden stuff, when he might easily grow them on his own patch of ground,—these and many other incidents of improvidence explain the constant dependence of the negro upon his employer and his creditor. There are, of course, notable exceptions where negroes have accumulated property through diligent attention and careful oversight. These are all the more notable when it is remembered that the education of the negro has directed his energies to the honors of the learned professions rather than to the commonplace virtues of ownership, and that one great practical experiment in thrift—the Freedman's Bank—went down through dishonesty and incapacity. With the more recent development of the remarkable institutions of Hampton and Tuskegee and their emphasis on manual training and property accumulation, it is to be expected that these basic qualities of intelligence and independence will receive practical and direct encouragement.

Coöperation is the third and capital equipment for attaining the rights of citizenship. There are two forms of coöperation—a lower and a higher. The lower is that of the chief or the boss who marshals his ignorant followers through fear or spoils. The higher is that of self-government where those who join together do so through their own intelligence and mutual confidence. In the lower form there are personal jealousies and factional contests which prevent united action under elected leaders. Negro bosses and foremen are more despotic than white bosses. The Colored Farmers' Alliance depended upon a white man for leadership. The white "carpet-baggers" organized the negro vote in the reconstruction period. The negro was in this low stage of coöperation because he was jealous or distrustful of his fellow-negro and could rally together only under the banner of a leader whom he could not depose. With the growth of intelligence and moral character there comes a deepening sense of the need of organization as well as leaders of their own race whom they can trust. The most hopeful indication of progress for the negroes is the large number of voluntary religious, beneficial, and insurance societies whose membership is limited to those of their own color.

Liberty has always come through organization. The free cities of Europe were simply the guilds of peasants and merchants who organized to protect themselves against the feudal lords and bishops. Latterly they gained a voice in parliaments as the "third estate" and established our modern representative democracy. The modern trade unions have become a power far in excess of their numbers through the capacity of the workman to organize. With the modest beginnings of self-organization among negroes the way is opening for their more effective participation in the higher opportunities of our civilization.

Counties having a Larger Proportion of Negroes in 1900 than in 1880

The negro trade unionist has not as yet shown the organizing capacity of other races. Only among the mine workers, the longshoremen, and bricklayers are they to be found in considerable numbers, although the carpenters have negro organizers. But in most of these cases the negro is being organized by the white man not so much for his own protection as for the protection of the white workman. If the negro is brought to the position of refusing to work for lower wages than the white man he has taken the most difficult step in organization; for the labor union requires, more than any other economic or business association in modern life, reliance upon the steadfastness of one's fellows. Unfortunately, when the negro demands the same wages as white men, his industrial inferiority leads the employer to take white men in his place, and here again we see how fundamental is manual and technical intelligence as a basis for other progress.

It must not be inferred because we have emphasized these qualities of intelligence—manliness and coöperation as preparatory to political rights—that the negro race should be deprived of the suffrage until such time as its members acquire these qualities. Many individuals have already acquired them. To exclude such individuals from the suffrage is to shut the door of hope to all. An honest educational test honestly enforced on both whites and blacks is the simplest rough-and-ready method for measuring the progress of individuals in these qualities of citizenship. There is no problem before the American people more vital to democratic institutions than that of keeping the suffrage open to the negro and at the same time preparing the negro to profit by the suffrage.

Neither should the negro be excluded from the higher education. Leadership is just as necessary in a democracy as in a tribe. Self-government is not suppression of leaders but coöperation with them. The true leader is one who knows his followers because he has suffered with them, but who can point the way out and inspire them with confidence. He feels what they feel, but can state what they cannot express. He is their spokesman, defender, and organizer. Not a social class nor a struggling race can reach equality with other classes and races until its leaders can meet theirs on equal terms. It cannot depend on others, but must raise up leaders from its own ranks. This is the problem of higher education—not that scholastic education that ends in itself, but that broad education that equips for higher usefulness. If those individuals who are competent to become lawyers, physicians, teachers, preachers, organizers, guides, innovators, experimenters, are prevented from getting the right education, then there is little hope for progress among the race as a whole, in the intelligence, manliness, and coöperation needed for self-government.

Growth of Negro Population.—After the census of 1880 it was confidently asserted that the negro population was increasing more rapidly than the white population. But these assertions, since the census of 1890, have disappeared. It then became apparent that the supposed increase from 1870 to 1880 was based on a defective count in 1870, the first census after emancipation. In reality the negro element, including mulattoes, during the one hundred and ten years of census taking, has steadily declined in proportion to the white element. Although negroes in absolute numbers have increased from 757,000 in 1790 to 4,442,000 in 1860, and 8,834,000 in 1900, yet in 1790 they were one-fifth of the total population; in 1860 they were one-seventh and in 1900 only one-ninth.

It is naturally suggested that this relative decrease in negro population has been owing to the large immigration of whites, but the inference is unwarranted. In the Southern states the foreign element has increased less rapidly than the native white element, yet it is in the Southern states that the negro is most clearly falling behind. In the twenty years from 1880 to 1900 the whites in eighteen Southern states without the aid of foreign immigration increased 57 per cent and the negroes only 33 per cent. In only six Southern states, West Virginia, Florida, Alabama, Mississippi, Oklahoma, and Arkansas, have the negroes, during the past ten years, increased more rapidly than the whites, and in only three of these states, Alabama, Mississippi, and Arkansas, was the relative increase significant. In but two states, South Carolina and Mississippi, does the negro element predominate, and in another state, Louisiana, a majority were negroes in 1890, but a majority were whites in 1900. "At the beginning of the nineteenth century the Southern negroes were increasing much faster than the Southern whites. At the end of it they were increasing only about three-fifths as fast."

This redistribution of negroes is an interesting and significant fact regarding the race and has a bearing on its future. Two movements are taking place, first to the fertile bottom lands of the Southern states, second to the cities, both North and South. Mr. Carl Kelsey has shown this movement to the lowlands in an interesting way. He has prepared a geological map of Alabama, which with Mississippi has received the largest accession of negroes, and has shown the density of negro population according to the character of the soil. In this map it appears that the prairie and valley regions contain a proportion of 50 per cent to 90 per cent negroes, while the sand hill and pine levels contain only 10 per cent to 50 per cent, and the piedmont or foothill region less than 10 per cent. A similar segregation is found in other Southern states, especially the alluvial districts of Mississippi and Arkansas. In these fertile sections toward which the negroes gravitate, the crops are enormous, and Mr. Kelsey points out a curious misconception in the census summary, wherein the inference is drawn that negroes are better farmers than whites because they raise larger crops. "No wonder the negroes' crops are larger," when the whites farm the hill country and the negroes till the delta, which "will raise twice as much cotton per acre as the hills." Furthermore the negro, whether tenant or owner, is under the close supervision of a white landlord or creditor, who in self-protection keeps control of him, whereas the white farmer is left to succeed or fail without expert guidance.

The migration of negroes to the cities is extremely significant. In ten Southern states the proportion of the colored population was almost exactly the same in 1890 as it had been in 1860,—namely, 36 per cent,—yet in sixteen cities of those states, as shown by Mr. Hoffman, the colored proportion increased from 19 per cent in 1860 to 29 per cent in 1890. This relative increase, however, did not continue after 1890, for, according to the census of 1900, the proportion of negroes in those cities was still 29 per cent. During the past decade the negroes have increased relatively faster in Northern cities. The white population of Chicago increased threefold from 1880 to 1900, and the colored population fivefold. The white population of Philadelphia during the same period increased 50 per cent and the colored population 100 per cent. In the thirty-eight largest cities of the country the negro population in ten years increased 38 per cent and the white population, including foreign immigration, increased 33 per cent. In thirty Northern and border cities during the past census decade the negroes gained 167,000, and in twenty Southern cities they gained 80,000.

The Southern whites also are moving from the South, and in larger proportions than the negroes, though the movement of both is small. In 1900, 7 per cent of the whites of Southern birth lived in the North and West and only 4.3 per cent of the negroes of Southern birth. But the negroes who go North go to the cities, and the whites to the country. Three-fifths (58 per cent) of these northbound negroes moved to the larger cities and only one-fourth (26 per cent) of the northbound whites.

The accompanying map, derived from the census of 1900, shows clearly both of these movements of negro population. The shaded areas indicate the counties where negroes formed a larger proportion of the population in 1900 than they did twenty years earlier, in 1880. Here can be seen the movement to the low and fertile lands of the South and the cities of the North and South. There are but two areas in California and Colorado, not included on the map, where the population of negroes has increased, and one of these contains the city of Los Angeles.

Were the negroes in the cities to scatter through all the sections, the predominating numbers of the white element might have an elevating influence, but, instead, the negroes congregate in the poorer wards, where both poverty and vice prevail. Hoffman has shown that two-thirds of the negroes in Chicago live in three wards, which contain all the houses of ill-fame in that part of the city. The same is true of Philadelphia, Boston, and Cincinnati. In these sections negro prostitution has become an established institution, catering to the Italian and other lower grades of immigrants, and supporting in idleness many negro men as solicitors.

We have seen that the negro population has not kept pace with the native white population. The reason is found in the smaller excess of births over deaths. Statistics of births are almost entirely lacking in the United States. Statistics of deaths are complete for only portions of Northern states and a few Southern cities, containing, in 1900, in all, 27,500,000 whites and 1,180,000 negroes. Of this number, 20,500,000 whites and 1,100,000 negroes lived in cities, so that the showing which the census is able to give is mainly for cities North and South and for rural sections only in the North. It appears that for every 1000 colored persons living in these cities the deaths in 1900 were 31.1, while for every 1000 white persons the deaths were only 17.9. That is to say, the colored death-rate was 73 per cent greater than the white death-rate.

In the rural districts there was much less difference. The colored death-rate was 19.1 and the white death-rate 15.3, a colored excess of 25 per cent.

Morals and Environment.—In explaining the excessive colored mortality there are two classes of opinions. One explains it by social conditions, the other by race traits. The one points to environment, the other to moral character. The one is socialistic, the other individualistic. These different views exist among colored people themselves, and one of the encouraging signs is the scientific and candid interest in the subject taken by them under the leadership of Atlanta University. A colored physician who takes the first view states his case forcibly:—

"Is it any wonder that we die faster than our white brother when he gets the first and best attention, while we are neglected on all sides? They have the best wards and treatment at the hospital, while we must take it second hand or not at all; they have all the homes for the poor and friendless, we have none; they have a home for fallen women, we have none; they have the public libraries where they can get and read books on hygiene and other subjects pertaining to health, we have no such privileges; they have the gymnasiums where they can go and develop themselves physically, we have not; they have all the parks where they and their children can go in the hot summer days and breathe the pure, cool air, but for fear we might catch a breath of that air and live, they put up large signs, which read thus, 'For white people only'; they live in the best homes, while we live in humble ones; they live in the cleanest and healthiest parts of the city, while we live in the sickliest and filthiest parts of the city; the streets on which they live are cleaned once and twice a day, the streets on which we live are not cleaned once a month, and some not at all; besides, they have plenty of money with which they can get any physician they wish, any medicine they need, and travel for their health when necessary; all of these blessings we are deprived of. Now, my friends, in the face of all these disadvantages, do you not think we are doing well to stay here as long as we do?"

Another colored writer, less eloquent, but not less accurate, in summarizing the statistics collected under the guidance of Atlanta University concludes:—

"Overcrowding in tenements and houses occupied by colored people does not exist to any great extent, and is less than was supposed.

"In comparison with white women, an excess of colored women support their families, or contribute to the family support, by occupation which takes them much of their time from home, to the neglect of their children.

"Environment and the sanitary condition of houses are not chiefly responsible for the excessive mortality among colored people.

"Ignorance and disregard of the laws of health are responsible for a large proportion of this excessive mortality."

It is pointed out by these colored students and by many others that the excessive mortality of colored people is owing to pulmonary consumption, scrofula, and syphilis, all of which are constitutional; and to infant mortality due also to constitutional and congenital disease. The census of 1900 reports for a portion of the Northern states that for every 1000 white children under five years of age there were 49.7 deaths in one year, and for every 1000 colored children under five years there were 118.5 deaths, an excess of negro infant mortality of 137 per cent. The census also reports that negro deaths in cities owing to consumption are proportionately 2.8 times as many as white deaths, deaths owing to pneumonia are 89 per cent greater, while deaths owing to contagious causes, such as measles, scarlet fever, diphtheria, are but slightly greater or actually less than the white deaths in proportion to population. In the city of Charleston, where mortality statistics of negroes were compiled before the war, it has been shown that from 1822 to 1848 the colored death-rate from consumption was a trifle less than the white, but since 1865 the white mortality from that cause has decreased 38 per cent, while the negro mortality has increased 70 per cent. The death-rates from consumption in Charleston in 1900 were 189.8 for 100,000 whites and 647.7 for 100,000 negroes, an excess of 241 per cent. The lowest negro death-rate reported from consumption in cities is 378.5 for Memphis, but in that city the white death-rate from the same cause is 169.9, a negro excess of 123 per cent.

At a conference held at Atlanta University, Professor Harris, of Fisk University, concluded:—

"I have now covered the ground to which our excessive death-rate is mainly due; namely, pulmonary diseases, especially consumption and pneumonia, scrofula, venereal diseases, and infant mortality. If we eliminate these diseases, our excessive death-rate will be a thing of the past.... While I do not depreciate sanitary regulations and a knowledge of hygienic laws, I am convinced that a *sine qua non* of a change for the better in the negro's physical condition is a higher social morality.... From the health reports of all our large Southern cities we learn that a considerable amount of our infant mortality is due to inanition, infantile debility, and infantile marasmus. Now what is the case in regard to these diseases? The fact is that they are not diseases at all, but merely the names of symptoms due to enfeebled constitutions and congenital diseases, inherited from parents suffering from the effects of sexual immorality and debauchery.... It is true that much of the moral laxity which exists among us to-day arose out of slavery.... But to explain it is not to excuse it. It is no longer our misfortune as it was before the war; it is our sin, the wages of which is our excessive number of deaths.... The presence of tubercular and scrofulous diseases, consumption, syphilis, and leprosy, has caused the weaker nations of the earth to succumb before the rising tide of Christian civilization.... The history of nations teaches us that neither war, nor famine, nor pestilence, exterminates them so completely as do sexual vices."

CHAPTER IV

NINETEENTH CENTURY ADDITIONS

It is only since the year 1820 that the government of the United States has kept a record of alien passengers arriving in this country. For several years following 1820 the immigration was so slight as to be almost negligible. It was not until 1820 that there were more than 20,000 arrivals. So accustomed have we become to large figures of immigration that nothing less than 100,000 seems worth noting, and this figure was not reached until 1842. Since then there have been only four years of less than 100,000, and two of these were years of the Civil War.

A striking fact which first attracts the attention of one who examines the statistics since 1840 is the close sympathy between immigration and the industrial prosperity and depression of this country. Indeed, so close is the connection that many who comment on the matter have held that immigration during the past century has been strictly an industrial or economic phenomenon, depending on the opportunities in this country, and that the religious and political causes which stimulated earlier immigration no longer hold good.

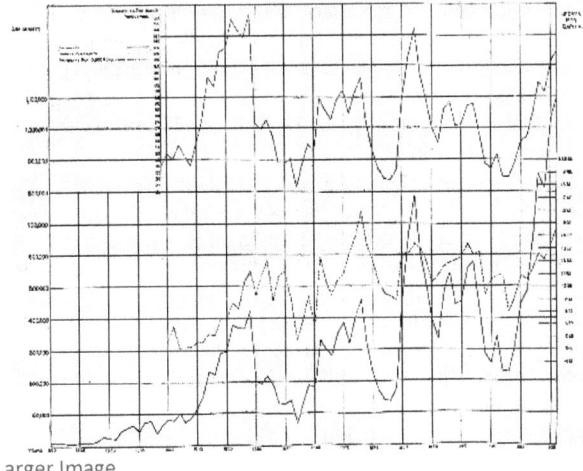

Larger Image

Movement of Immigrants, Imports of Merchandise per capita, and Immigrants per 10,000 Population—1800 to 1906.

A curved line on the accompanying chart has been drawn so as to show the relative numbers of immigrants since 1800, and another line shows the movement of imports of merchandise per capita of the population. The latter, except for tariff changes, is a fair index of the cycles of prosperity and depression. By following these two lines on the chart we notice the coincidence is close, except for a few years prior to the Civil War. Both movements reached high points in 1873, and fell to very low points in 1879; then rose in 1882 and fell in 1885; then reached another high point in 1892 and a low point in 1897; and finally, the present period of prosperity and heavy imports brings the largest immigration in the history of the country.

In following the history of immigration by races we shall see to what extent the alleged coincidence between prosperity and immigration may be counted as a social law. Probably in the middle of the century it was not so much the opportunities for employment in this country as it was conditions in Europe that drove people to our shores. When we come to inquire as to the nationalities which constituted immigration at that period, we shall find what these causes were. In 1846 occurred the unparalleled potato rot in Ireland, when the year's crop of what had become the sole food staple of the peasantry of that island was entirely lost. The peasants had been reduced to subsistence on the cheapest of all staples through the operations of a system of landlordism scarcely ever paralleled on a large scale as a means of exploiting tenants. It was found that land used for potatoes would support three times the number of people as the same land sown to wheat, and the small tenants or the cotter peasants paid the landlord a higher rent than could be obtained from larger cultivators. Reduced to a diet of potatoes by an economic system imposed by an alien race, the Irish people are one of the many examples which we find throughout our studies of a subject people driven to emigration by the economic injustices of a dominant race. We shall find the same at a later time in Austria-Hungary, whence the conquered Slav peoples are fleeing from the discrimination and impositions of the ruling Magyar. We shall find it in Russia, whence the Jew, the Finn, and the German are escaping from the oppression of the Slav; and we shall find it in Turkey, whence the Armenian and the Syrian flee from the exactions of the Turk. Just so was it in Ireland in the latter half of the decade, 1840 to 1850, and the contention of the apologist for England that the famine which drove the Irish across the seas was an act of God, is but a weak effort to charge to a higher power the sufferings of a heartless system devised to convert the utmost life and energy of a subject race into gold for their exploiters. Much more nearly true of the part played by the Divine hand in this catastrophe is the report of the Society of Friends in Ireland, saying that the mysterious dispensation with which their country had been visited was "a means permitted by an All-wise Providence to exhibit more strikingly the unsound state of its social condition."

Thus we have an explanation of the incentives under which, even in a period of industrial depression in this country, the unfortunate Irish flocked hither. It is true that the population of Ireland had increased during the century preceding the famine at a rate more rapid than that of any other country of Europe. It was 3,000,000 in 1790, and over 8,000,000 in the year of the famine. At the present time it is only 5,000,000. The potato, above all other crops, enables the cultivator to live from hand to mouth, and coupled with a landlord system which takes away all above mere subsistence, this "de-moralizing esculent" aided the apparent overpopulation. Certainly the dependence of an entire people on a single crop was a most precarious condition.

During the five years, 1846 to 1850, more than a million and a quarter of Irish emigrants left the ports of the United Kingdom, and during the ten years, 1845 to 1855, more than a million and a quarter came to the United States. So great a number could not have found means of transportation had it not been for the enormous contributions of government and private societies for assistance. Here began that exportation of paupers on a large scale against which our country has protested and finally legislated. Even this enormous migration was not greatly in excess of the number that actually perished from starvation or from the diseases incident thereto. The Irish migration since that time has never reached so high a point, although it made a second great advance in 1882, succeeding another famine, and it has now fallen far below that of eastern races of Europe. Altogether the total Irish immigration of over four million since 1821 places that race second of the contributors to our foreign-born population, and, compared with its own numbers, it leads the world, for in sixty years it has sent to us half as many people as it contained at the time of its greatest population. Scarcely another country has sent more than one-fifth.

Looking over a period of nearly three centuries, it is probably true that the Germans have crossed the ocean in larger numbers than any other race. We have already noted the large migration during the eighteenth century, and the official records show that since 1820 there have entered our ports more than 5,200,000 Germans, while Ireland was sending 4,000,000 and Great Britain 3,300,000.

The German migration of the nineteenth century was quite distinct in character from that of the preceding century. The colonial migration was largely induced on religious grounds, but that of the past century was political and economic, with at first a notable prominence of materialism respecting religion. From the time of the Napoleonic wars to the revolution of 1848, the governments of Germany were despotic in character, supporting an established church, while at the same time the marvellous growth of the universities produced a class of educated liberals. In the revolution of 1848 these took a leading part, and although constitutional governments were then established, yet those who had been prominent in the popular uprisings found their position intolerable under the reactionary governments that followed. The political exiles sought America, bringing their liberalism in politics and religion, and forming with their descendants in American cities an intellectual aristocracy. They sprang from the middle classes of Germany, and latterly, when the wars with Austria and France had provoked the spirit of militarism, thousands of peasants looked to emigration for escape from military service. The severe industrial depression of 1873-79 added a powerful contributing cause. Thus there were two periods when German migration culminated; first in 1854, on political grounds, second in 1882, on military and economic grounds. Since the latter date a significant decline has ensued, and the present migration of 32,000 from Germany is mainly the remnants of families seeking here their relatives. A larger number of German immigrants, 55,000, comes from Austria-Hungary and Russia, those from the latter country being driven from the Baltic provinces and the Volga settlements by the "Russianizing" policy of the Slav.

The Changing Character of European Immigration.—Besides the Germans and the Irish, the races which contributed the largest numbers of immigrants during the middle years of the nineteenth century were the English and Scandinavian. After the decline during the depression of 1879 there was an increase of all those races in 1882, a year when nearly 800,000 immigrants arrived. At about that time began a remarkable change in the character of immigration destined to produce profound consequences.

This change was the rapid shifting of the sources of immigration from Western to Eastern and Southern Europe. A line drawn across the continent of Europe from northeast to southwest, separating the Scandinavian Peninsula, the British Isles, Germany, and France from Russia, Austria-Hungary, Italy, and Turkey, separates countries not only of distinct races but also of distinct civilizations. It separates Protestant Europe from Catholic Europe; it separates countries of representative institutions and popular government from absolute monarchies; it separates lands where education is universal from lands where illiteracy predominates; it separates manufacturing countries, progressive agriculture, and skilled labor from primitive hand industries, backward agriculture, and unskilled labor; it separates an educated, thrifty peasantry from a peasantry scarcely a single generation removed from serfdom; it separates Teutonic races from Latin, Slav, Semitic, and Mongolian races. When the sources of American immigration are shifted from the Western countries so nearly allied to our own, to Eastern countries so remote in the main attributes of Western civilization, the change is one that should challenge the attention of every citizen. Such a change has occurred, and it needs only a comparison of the statistics of immigration for the year 1882 with those of 1902 and 1906 to see its extent. While the total number of immigrants from Europe and Asiatic Turkey was approximately equal in 1882 and 1902, as shown in the accompanying table, yet in 1882 Western Europe furnished 87 per cent of the immigrants and in 1902 only 22 per cent, while the share of Southeastern Europe and Asiatic Turkey increased from 13 per cent in 1882 to 78 per cent in 1902. During twenty years the immigration of the Western races most nearly related to those which have fashioned American institutions declined more than 75 per cent, while the immigrants of Eastern and Southern races, untrained in self-government, increased nearly sixfold. For the year 1906 the proportions remain the same, although in the four years the total immigration had increased two-thirds.

IMMIGRATION FROM EUROPE AND ASIATIC TURKEY BY COUNTRIES, 1882, 1902, 1906

	1882 NUMBER	1882 PER CENT	1902 NUMBER	1902 PER CENT	1905 NUMBER	1905 PER CENT
Total Europe and Asiatic Turkey	647,082	100	622,987	100	1,024,719	100
Great Britain and Ireland	179,423	27.7	46,036	7.4	102,241	10.0
Belgium	1,431	.2	2,577	.4	5,099	.5

Denmark	11,618	1.8	5,660	.9	7,741	.8
France	6,003	.9	5,117	.8	9,386	.9
Germany	250,630	38.7	26,304	4.2	37,564	3.7
Netherlands	9,517	1.1	2,284	.4	4,946	.5
Norway	29,101	4.5	17,404	2.8	21,730	2.1
Sweden	64,607	10.0	30,894	5.0	23,310	2.3
Switzerland	10,884	1.7	2,344	.4	3,846	.4
Total Western Europe	563,174	87.0	136,620	22.0	215,863	21.7
Italy	32,159	5.0	178,375	28.6	273,120	26.7
Portugal	42		5,307	.9	8,517	.8
Spain	378		975	.1	1,921	.1
Austria-Hungary	29,150	4.5	171,989	27.6	265,138	25.9
Russia	21,590	3.3	107,347	17.2	215,665	21.0
Greece	73		8,104	1.3	19,489	1.9
Roumania	77		7,196	1.2	4,476	.5
Servia, Bulgaria, and Montenegro			851		4,666	.5
Turkey in Europe	86		187		9,510	.9
Turkey in Asia	82		6,223	1.0	6,354	.6
Total Southern and Eastern Europe and Asiatic Turkey	83,637	13.0	486,367	78.0	808,856	78.9

Italians.—It was at this period that Italian immigration first became noticeable. Prior to 1880 this stream had been but the merest trickle, which now has become the greatest of all the foreign tributaries to our population. In 1873 the Italians for the first time reached 8000 in number, but they fell to 3000 in 1876 and so continued in moderate proportions, but suddenly in 1880 jumped to 12,000, and in 1882 to 32,000. Falling off again with the industrial depression to 13,000 in 1885, they reached 76,000 in 1891, and then with another depression to 35,000 in 1895 they have now gone forward by leaps to the high mark of 287,000. The Italians seem destined to rival the Germans and Irish as the leading contributors to our social amalgam. Of course only a small part are as yet women and children, but this is because the immigration is in its early and pioneer stages. The women and children follow rapidly when the men have saved enough money to send for them. One-fourth of the emigration is on tickets and money furnished by friends and relatives in the United States.

The immigrants from Italy differ from those from Austria, Russia, Hungary, and Ireland, in that they are not driven forth by the oppressions of a dominant race, but as a result of the economic and political conditions of a united people. This does not indeed exclude oppression as a cause of expatriation, but it transfers the oppression from that of one race to that of one class upon another. By far the larger portion of Italian immigration comes from the southern provinces and from Sicily, where the power of the landlords is greatest. In these provinces of large estates held by the nobility, the rents have been forced to the highest notch, an orange garden paying as high as $160 per year per acre, and the leases are short, so that the tenant has little to encourage improvement. In many cases the land is rented by large capitalist farmers, who raise therefrom cattle, wheat, and olives, and are prosperous men. But their prosperity is extracted from the miserable wages of their laborers. The agricultural laborer gets from 8 cents to 32 cents a day through the year and 10 cents to 38 cents through the summer. Unskilled laborers get 25 cents to 50 cents a day, and such skilled trades as masons and carpenters get only 27 cents to $1.40 a day. This wide range of wages corresponds generally with the South and North, the lowest rates being in the South and the highest toward the North. In France and England wages are two and one-half times higher than in Italy, while in Germany they are about 30 per cent to 50 per cent higher.

Nor must it be supposed that the cost of living is low to correspond with the low wages. This is largely owing to the exaggerated system of indirect taxes. Although wheat is a staple crop, yet the peasants eat corn in preference, because, for a given expenditure, it gives a stronger sense of repletion. Of wheat and corn meal together the Italian peasant eats in a year only three-fourths as much as the inmate of an English poorhouse. Of meat the peasant in Apulia gets no more than ten pounds a year, while the English workhouse pauper gets fifty-seven pounds. The local taxes on flour, bread, and macaroni are as high as 10 or 15 per cent of the value, and the state tax on imported wheat is nearly 50 per cent of its value. The consumption of sugar has decreased one-fourth since heavy duties were imposed to protect native beet sugar, and it averages barely over five pounds per head. The consumption in the United States is sixty-five pounds per head. The iniquitous salt tax raises the price of salt from eleven pounds for two cents to one pound for two cents, and the peasants sometimes cook their corn meal in sea water, although this is smuggling. What the peasants lack in grain and meat they strive to supply by vegetables, and the proportion of vegetables, peas, and beans consumed is greater than that for any other country of Europe. The peasants drink no beer, spirits, tea, nor coffee, but the average annual consumption of wine is twenty gallons a head. Food alone costs the peasants 85 per cent of their wages, whereas it costs the German peasant 62 per cent and the American workman 41 per cent. The poor and working classes pay over one-half the taxes, amounting, even without wine, to 10 or 20 per cent of their wages. There are in the south and Sardinia some 13,000 sales of land a year on distress for non-payment of taxes, and the expropriated owners become tenants. Several villages in Southern Italy have been almost wholly abandoned and one village has recently announced its intention of removing itself entire to one of the South American republics. The rich escape taxation, which is laid largely on consumption. Besides the state tax on imports, each city and town has its *octroi*, or import tax, on everything brought into the city. These "protective duties rob the poor to fill the pockets of the rich landlord and manufacturer." Since 1870 wealth has increased 17 per cent and taxes 30 per cent. Taxes are nearly one-fifth of the nation's income, against one-twelfth in Germany, one-sixteenth in England, and one-fifteenth in the United States. Wages rose from 1860 to 1885, but since 1890 they have fallen.

The army and navy are the greatest drain on the resources of the people. They cost one-fourth more of the national income than do the armies and navies of France and Germany. Eighty million dollars a year for military expenditures in Italy is over 5 per cent of the income of the people, whereas $194,000,000 for the same purpose in the United States is less than 2 per cent of our incomes. In the Triple Alliance of Germany,

Austria, and Italy, the latter country crushes its peasants in order to make a showing by the side of its wealthier partners. The army takes every able-bodied peasant from industry into barracks and drills for two years of his best vigor. But the long line of exposed coast and the general military situation in Europe make it unlikely that Italy for many years can shake off this incubus.

In addition to all these economic and political causes of pressure, there is another cause of a more profound nature, the rapid growth of population. Strange as it may seem, the very poverty of Italy increases the tendency to a high birth-rate, and the rate is highest in the very districts where illiteracy and poverty are greatest. Only the great number of deaths produced by poverty and lack of sanitation prevents the increase of population from exceeding that of the more rapidly growing countries of Germany, Great Britain, and Scandinavia. It is not among those classes and nations, like the middle classes and the thrifty people of France, that the largest number of children are born, but it is among those ignorant and low-standard peoples to whom the future offers no better prospect for their children than for themselves. Early marriages and large families are both a result and a cause of poverty. Parts of Lombardy and Venetia have a thicker population than any other European country except Belgium, which is really not a country, but a manufacturing centre of Europe. The density of population in Italy is in excess of that of Germany, France, India, and even China. It is exceeded only by the islands of Great Britain and Japan, and the states of Rhode Island and Massachusetts. Emigration is the only immediate relief from this congestion. All other remedies which operate through raising the intelligence and the standards of living require years for appreciable results, but meanwhile the persistent birth-rate crowds new competitors into the new openings and multiplies the need of economic and political reforms before they can be put into effect. Emigration is a relief ready at hand, but it is not a lessening of population. For many years to come Italy will furnish a surplus population to overflow to America. Emigration is also a means of revenue for the mother country. For it is estimated that the peasants in foreign countries send back to their families and relatives $30,000,000 to $80,000,000 each year, and many of them return with what to them is a fortune, and with new ideas of industry and progress, to purchase and improve a farm and cottage for their declining years. It is said that already there are several small country towns in Southern Italy which have risen from squalor to something of prosperity through the money and influence of those who have come home. This temporary emigration is probably over 150,000 each year going abroad or to adjoining countries expecting to return.

Besides this temporary emigration there is an equally large permanent emigration. This is of two kinds, almost as entirely distinct from each other as the emigration from two separate nations. The North Italian is an educated, skilled artisan, coming from a manufacturing section and largely from the cities. He is Teutonic in blood and appearance. The South Italian is an illiterate peasant from the great landed estates, with wages less than one-third his northern compatriot. He descends with less mixture from the ancient inhabitants of Italy. Unhappily for us, the North Italians do not come to the United States in considerable numbers, but they betake themselves to Argentina, Uruguay, and Brazil in about the same numbers as the South Italians come to us. It is estimated that in those three countries there are 3,000,000 Italians in a total population of 23,000,000, and they are mainly derived from the north of Italy. Surrounded by the unenterprising Spanish and Portuguese, they have shown themselves to be the industrial leaders of the country. Some of the chief buildings, banks, flour mills, textile mills, and a majority of the wheat farms of Argentina belong to Italians. They are one-third of the population of Buenos Ayres and own one-half of the commercial capital of that city. They become lawyers, engineers, members of parliament, and an Italian by descent has been president of the Republic of Argentina, while other Italians have been ministers of war and education. While these North Italians, with their enterprise, intelligence, and varied capacities, go to South America, we receive the South Italians, who are nearly the most illiterate of all immigrants at the present time, the most subservient to superiors, the lowest in their standards of living, and at the same time the most industrious and thrifty of all common laborers.

Aliens awaiting Admission at Ellis Island

Austria-Hungary.—Next to that from Italy the immigration from the Austro-Hungarian Empire in recent decades has reached the largest dimensions. While Italy sent 273,000 people in 1906, Austria-Hungary sent 265,000 in that year and 276,000 the year before. Like the immigration from Italy, this increase has occurred since 1880. Prior to that date the largest number reported from Austria-Hungary was 9000 in 1874.

While these figures compare with those of the Italians, yet, unlike the Italians, they refer to a congeries of races and languages distinct one from another. The significance of Austro-Hungarian immigration is revealed only when we analyze it by races. The race map of this empire shows at once the most complicated social mosaic of all modern nations. Here we see, not that mixture of races and assimilation of language which in our own country has evolved a vigorous, united people, but a juxtaposition of hostile races and a fixity of language held together only by the outside pressure of Russia, Germany, Italy, and Turkey. This conflict of races has made the politics of the empire nearly incomprehensible to foreigners, and has aggravated the economic inequalities which drive the unprivileged masses to emigrate.

Not only are there in Austria-Hungary five grand divisions of the human family,—the German, the Slav, the Magyar, the Latin, and the Jew,—but these are again subdivided. In the northern mountainous and hilly sections are 13,000,000 Slavic peoples, the Czechs, or Bohemians, with their closely related Moravians, and the Slavic Slovaks, Poles, and Ruthenians (known also as Russniaks); while in the southern hills and along the Adriatic are another 4,000,000 Slavs, the Croatians, Servians, Dalmatians, and Slovenians. Between these divisions on the fertile plains 8,000,000 Magyars and 10,000,000 Germans have thrust themselves as the dominant races. To the southwest are nearly a million Italians, and in the east 2,500,000 Latinized Slavs, the Roumanians. The Slavs are in general the conquered peoples, with a German and Magyar nobility owning their land, making their laws, and managing their administration. The northern Slavs are subject to Austria and Hungary, and the Ruthenians suffer a double subjection, for they were the serfs of their fellow-Slavs, the Poles, whom they continue to hate, and in whose longings for a reunited Poland they do not participate. The southern Slavs and Roumanians are subject to Hungary. The Roumanians are a widespread and disrupted nationality of Slavs, conquered by the Romans, from whom they imperfectly took their language, but now distributed partly in independent kingdoms and partly under the dominion of the Magyars. The Croatians from the southwest mountains are among the finest specimens of physical manhood coming to our shores. They are a vigorous people, hating Hungary which owns them and calling themselves "Austrians" to ward off the name "Hun," by which Americans mistakenly designate them. The Magyars are the Asiactic conquerors who overran Europe ten centuries ago, and being repulsed by the Teutons to the west established themselves on the Slavs in the valley and plains of the Danube. Boasting a republican constitution a thousand years old they have not until the past year been compelled to share it with the people whom they subdued. Astute politicians and dashing military leaders, they are as careless in business as the Slavs, and the supremacy which they maintained in politics has slipped into the hands of the Jews in economics. In no other modern country has the Jew been so liberally treated, and in no other country have public and private finance come more completely under his control. Profiting by the Magyars' suppression of the Slavs, the Jew has monopolized the business opportunities denied to the Slovak and the Croatian, and with this leverage has quietly elbowed out the Magyar himself. No longer is the Magyar the dominant race, and in the past year he has contributed to America more immigrants than any branch of his conquered Slavs. In the Austrian dominions of former Poland the Jew likewise has become the financier, and both the Ruthenian and the Pole, unable to rise under their burden of debt, contribute their more enterprising peasants to America.

By a perverse system of representative government, based on representation of classes both in Austria and in Hungary, the great landowners and wealthy merchants have heretofore elected three-fourths of the parliaments, but recently in both countries the emperor has granted universal manhood suffrage. The peasant Slavs will henceforth be on equal footing with the German, the Magyar, and the Jew, and whether out of the belated equality of races there will come equality of economic opportunity remains to be seen. For the past few years the emigration from the unfortunate dual empire has amazingly increased.

With all of this confusing medley of races, with this diversity of Greek and Roman Catholicism and Judaism, with this history of race oppression and hatred, it is not surprising that the immigrants should break out into factions and feuds wherever thrown together among us. It is the task of America to lift them to a patriotism which hitherto in their native land they could not know.

The earliest migration from Austria-Hungary was that of the Bohemians, the most highly educated and ardently patriotic of the Slavic people. After the revolution of 1848, when the Germans suppressed their patriotic uprising, students, professional men, and well-to-do peasants came to America and settled in New York, St. Louis, Milwaukee, Chicago, and in the rural districts of Texas, Wisconsin, Iowa, Minnesota, and California. Again, after the Austro-Prussian War of 1866, skilled laborers were added to the stream, and they captured a large part of the cigar-making industry of New York and the clothing trade of Chicago. Latterly recruits from the peasants and unskilled laborers sought the sections where the pioneers had located, learned the same trades, or joined the armies of common labor. In Chicago the Bohemian section is almost a self-governing city, with its own language, industries, schools, churches, and newspapers. After a slight decline there is again an increasing flow of immigrants, the number in 1906 being 13,000. Those who come bring their families, and few return. In these earlier days the Polish and Hungarian Jews also began their migration, following the steps of their German precursors.

In the decade of the eighties the increase of immigration from Austria-Hungary was first that of the Poles, now numbering 44,000, then the Magyars, now 43,000, then the Slovaks, now 37,000. In the latter part of the nineties the Southern Slavs—Croatians and Slovenians—suddenly took up their burden, and 43,000 of them came in 1906. Following them came the Ruthenians from the North, numbering 16,000 in 1906. Last of all, the Latinized Slavs, the Roumanians, began their flight from the Magyar, to the number of less than 400 in the year 1900, but swelling to 11,000 in 1906. Only 300 additional came from their own proper kingdom—Roumania. During all this period there has been also a considerable migration of Germans, reaching 35,000 in 1906.

In the face of this swollen migration the Hungarian government has at last taken alarm. They see even their own people, the Magyars, escaping. Recently the government has attempted to restrict the unrest by prohibiting advertisements or public speeches advocating emigration, by prohibiting the sale of tickets or solicitation by any one not holding a government license for the purpose, by contracting with a steamship line from their own Adriatic part of Fiume in order to reduce migration across the German and Italian frontiers. This may account for the decline of ten thousand immigrants from Austria-Hungary in 1906.

Practically the entire migration of the Slavic elements at the present time is that of peasants. In Croatia the forests have been depleted, and thousands of immigrant wood-choppers have sought the forests of our South and the railway construction of the West. The natural resources of Croatia are by no means inadequate, but the discriminating taxes and railway freight rates imposed by Hungary have prevented the development of these resources. The needed railways are not obtainable for the development of the mines and minerals of Croatia, and the peasants, unable to find employment at home, are allured by the advertisements of American steamships and the agents of American contractors.

So it is with the Slovak peasants and mine workers of the northern mountains and foothills. With agricultural wages only eighteen cents a day, they find employment in the American mines, rolling-mills, stock-yards, and railroad construction at $1.50 a day.

In addition to race discrimination, the blight of Austria-Hungary is landlordism. Considerable reforms, indeed, have been made in certain sections. The free alienation of landed property was adopted in the Austrian dominions in 1869, and in the following twelve years 42,000 new holdings were carved out of the existing peasant proprietorships in Bohemia. Similar transfers have occurred elsewhere, but even where this peasant ownership has gained, the enormous prices are an obstacle to economic independence. They compel the land-owning peasant to content himself with five to twelve acres, the size of four-fifths of the farms in Galicia. His eagerness to own land is his dread of the mere wage-earner's lot, which he no longer dreads when he lands in America. "The fear of falling from the social position of a peasant to that, immeasurably inferior, of a day laborer, is the great spur which drives over the seas alike the Slovak, the Pole, and the Ruthenian." These high rentals and fabulous values can exist only where wages and standards of living are at the bare subsistence level, leaving a heavy surplus for capitalization. They also exist as a result of most economical and minute cultivation, so that, with this training, the Bohemian or Polish farmer who takes up land in America soon becomes a well-to-do citizen.

Taxation, too, is unequal. For many years the government suffered deficits, the military expenses increased, and worst of all, the nobility were exempt from taxation. The latter injustice, however, was remedied by the revolution of 1848, and yet at the present time the great landowners pay much less than their proportionate share of the land-tax, to say nothing of the heavy taxes on consumption and industry.

As in other countries of low standards, the number of births is large in proportion to the inhabitants. For every one thousand persons in Hungary, there are forty-three births each year, a number exceeded by but one great country of Europe, Russia. Yet, with this large number of births, because the economic conditions are so onerous and the consequent deaths so frequent, the net increase is less than that of any other country except France. In Austria the births and deaths are less and the net increase greater, and they run close to those of prolific Italy.

In each of these countries the figures for births and deaths stand near those of the negroes in America, and like the negroes, two-fifths of the mortality is that of children under five years of age, whereas with other more favored countries and races this proportion is only one-fifth or one-fourth. It is not so much the overpopulation of Austria-Hungary that incites emigration as it is the poverty, ignorance, inequality, and helplessness that produce a seeming overpopulation. While these conditions continue, emigration will continue to increase, and the efforts of the Hungarian government to reduce it will not succeed.

Russia.—The Russian Empire is at the present time the third in the rank of contributors to American immigration. Russian immigration, like that of Italy and Austria-Hungary, is practically limited to the past two decades. In 1881 it first reached 10,000. In 1893 it was 42,000, and in 1906, 216,000.

The significant fact of this immigration is that it is only 2 per cent Russian and 98 per cent non-Russian. The Russian peasant is probably the most oppressed of the peasants of Europe, and though his recent uprising has aroused his intellect and disabused the former opinion of his stupidity, yet he has been so tied to the soil by his system of communism, his burden of taxes and debt and his subjection to landlords, that he is as yet immune to the fever of migration. In so far as he has moved from his native soil he has done so through the efforts of a despotic government to Russianize Siberia and the newly conquered regions of his own vast domain. On the other hand, the races which have abandoned the Russian Empire have been driven forth because they refused to submit to the policy which would by force assimilate them to the language or religion of the dominant race. Even the promises of the aristocracy under the fright of recent revolution have not mitigated the persecutions, and the number taking refuge in flight has doubled in four years. Foremost are the Jews, 125,000 in 1906, an increase from 37,000 four years ago; next the Poles, 46,000 in 1906; next 14,000 Lithuanians, 13,000 Finns, and 10,000 Germans. The Poles and Lithuanians are Slavic peoples long since conquered and annexed by the Russians. The Finns are a Teutonic people with a Mongol language; the Germans are an isolated branch of that race settled far to the east on the Volga River by invitation of the Czar more than one hundred years ago, or on the Baltic provinces adjoining Germany; while the Jews are the unhappy descendants of a race whom the Russians found in territory conquered during the past two centuries.

The Jews.—Russia, at present, sends us five-sixths of the Jewish immigration, but the other one-sixth comes from adjoining territory in Austria-Hungary and Roumania. About six thousand temporarily sojourn in England, and the Whitechapel district of East London is a reduced picture of the East Side, New York. During American history Jews have come hither from all countries of Europe. The first recorded immigration was that of Dutch Jews, driven from Brazil by the Portuguese and received by the Dutch government of New Amsterdam. The descendants of these earliest immigrants continue at the present time in their own peculiar congregation in lower New York City. Quite a large number of Portuguese and Spanish Jews, expelled from those countries in the time of Columbus, have contributed their descendants to America by way of Holland. The German Jews began their migration in small numbers during colonial times, but their greatest influx followed the Napoleonic wars and reached its height at the middle of the century. Prior to the last two decades so predominant were the German Jews that, to the ordinary American, all Jews were Germans. Strangely enough, the so-called Russian Jew is also a

German, and in Russia among the masses of people the words "German" and "Jew" also mean the same thing. Hereby hangs a tale of interest in the history of this persecuted race. Jews are known to have settled at the site of the present city of Frankfort in Southern Germany as early as the third century, when that town was a trading post on the Roman frontier. At the present time the region about Frankfort, extending south through Alsace, contains the major part of the German and French Jews. To this centre they flocked during the Middle Ages, and their toleration in this region throws an interesting light on the reasons for their persecution in other countries.

Under the Catholic polity following the crusades the Jew had no rights, and he could therefore gain protection only through the personal favor of emperor, king, or feudal lord. This protection was arbitrary and capricious, but it was always based on a pecuniary consideration. Unwittingly the Catholic Church, by its prohibition of usury to all believers, had thrown the business of money lending into the hands of the Jews, and since the Jew was neither inclined toward agriculture nor permitted to follow that vocation, his only sources of livelihood were trade and usury. The sovereigns of Europe who protected the Jews did so in view of the large sums which they could exact from their profits as usurers and traders. They utilized the Jews like sponges to draw from their subjects illicit taxes. When, therefore, the people gained power over their sovereigns, and the spirit of nationality arose, the Jew, without his former protector, was the object of persecution. England was the first country where this spirit of nationality emerged and the first to expel the Jews (1290); France followed a century later (1395); and Spain and Portugal two centuries later (1492 and 1495). But in Germany and other parts of the Holy Roman Empire political confusion and anarchy prevailed, and the emperor and petty sovereigns were able to continue their protection of the Jews.

Norwegian Italian Arabic
(From *The Home Missionary*)

The Russian people, at that time, were confined to the interior surrounding Moscow, but even before the crusades they had expelled the Jews. As rapidly as they conquered territory to the south from Turkey, or to the west from Poland, they carried forward the same hostility. There was only one country, Poland, in the centre of Europe, where the kings, desiring to build up their cities, invited the Jews, and hither the persecuted race fled from the East before the Russians, and latterly from the West, driven out by the Germans. When finally, a hundred years ago, the remnant of the Polish Empire was divided between Russia, Prussia, and Austria, the Jewish population in this favored area had become the largest aggregation of that people since the destruction of Jerusalem. To-day in certain of these provinces belonging to Russia the Jews number as high as one-sixth of the entire population, and more than half of that of several cities. Fifteen provinces taken from Poland and Turkey, extending 1500 miles along the border of Germany and Austria-Hungary and 240 miles in width, constitute to-day the "Pale of Settlement," the region where Jews are permitted to live. Here are found one-third of the world's 11,000,000 Jews. Here they formerly engaged in all lines of industry, including agriculture.

Now we come to the last great national uprising, like that which began in England six hundred years ago. The Russian serfs had been freed in 1861. But they were left without land or capital and were burdened by high rents and enormous taxes. The Jews became their merchants, middlemen, and usurers. Suddenly, in 1881, the peasants, oppressed and neglected by landlord and government, turned in their helplessness upon the intermediate cause of their misery, the Jew. The anti-Semitic riots of that year have perhaps never been exceeded in ferocity and indiscriminate destruction. Then began the migration to America. The next year the Russian government took up the persecution, and the notorious "May Orders" of 1882 were promulgated. These, at the instigation of the Greek Church, have been followed by orders more stringent, so that to-day, unless relieved by the terrorized promises of the Czar, the Jew is not permitted to foreclose a mortgage or to lease or purchase land; he cannot do business on Sundays or Christian holidays; he cannot hold office; he cannot worship or assemble without police permit; he must serve in the army, but cannot become an officer; he is excluded from schools and universities; he is fined for conducting manufactures and commerce; he is almost prohibited from the learned professions. While all other social questions are excluded from discussion, the anti-Semitic press is given free play, and the popular hatred of the Jew is stirred to frenzy by "yellow" journals. Only when this hatred breaks out in widespread riots does the news reach America, but the persecution is constant and relentless. The government and the army join with the peasants, for, true to the character of this versatile race, the Jews are leaders of the revolutionary and socialistic patriots who seek to overthrow the government and restore the land to the people.

Nor is this uprising confined to Russia. Galician Jews in the Austrian possessions of former Poland, where the Slavs bitterly complain of them as saloon-keepers and money-lenders, have suffered the persecutions of their race, and in the last ten years Roumania, a country of peasants adjoining Hungary and Russia, has adopted laws and regulations even more oppressive than those of her neighbor.

Thus it is that this marvellous and paradoxical race, the parent of philosophers, artists, reformers, martyrs, and also of the shrewdest exploiters of the poor and ignorant, has, in two decades, come to America in far greater numbers than in the two centuries preceding.

It should not be inferred that the Jews are a race of pure descent. Coming as they do from all sections and nations of Europe, they are truly cosmopolitan, and have taken on the language, customs, and modes of thought of the people among whom they live. More than this, in the course of centuries, their physical characteristics have departed from those of their Semitic cousins in the East, and they have become assimilated in blood with their European neighbors. In Russia, especially in the early centuries, native tribes were converted to Judaism and mingled with their proselyters. That which makes the Jew a peculiar people is not altogether the purity of his blood, but persecution, devotion to his religion, and careful training of his children. Among the Jews from Eastern Europe there are marked intellectual and moral differences. The Hungarian Jew, who emigrated earliest, is adventurous and speculative: the Southern Russian keeps few of the religious observances, is the most intellectual and socialistic, and most inclined to the life of a wage-earner; the Western Russian is orthodox and emotional, saves money, becomes a contractor and retail merchant; the Galician Jew is the poorest, whose conditions at home were the harshest, and he begins American life as a pedler. That which unites them all as a single people is their religious training and common language.

The Hebrew language is read and written by all the men and half of the women, but is not spoken except by a few especially orthodox Jews on Saturday. Hebrew is the language of business and correspondence, Yiddish the language of conversation, just as Latin in the Middle Ages was the official and international language, while the various peoples spoke each its own vernacular. The Yiddish spoken by the Russian Jews in America is scarcely a language—it is a jargon without syntax, conjugation, or declension. Its basis is sixty per cent German of the sixteenth century, showing the main origin of the people, and forty per cent the language of the countries whence they come.

That which most of all has made the Jew a cause of alarm to the peasants of Eastern Europe is the highest mark of his virtue, namely, his rapid increase in numbers. A high birth-rate, a low death-rate, a long life, place the Jew as far above the average as the negro is below the average. These two races are the two extremes of American race vitality. Says Ripley:—

"Suppose two groups of one hundred infants each, one Jewish, one of average American parentage (Massachusetts), to be born on the same day. In spite of the disparity of social conditions in favor of the latter, the chances, determined by statistical means, are that one-half of the Americans will die within forty-seven years; while the first half of the Jews will not succumb to disease or accident before the expiration of seventy-one years. The death-rate is really but little over half that of the average American population."

While the negro exceeds all races in the constitutional diseases of consumption and pneumonia, the Jew excels all in immunity from these diseases. His vitality is ascribed to his sanitary meat inspection, his sobriety, temperance, and self-control. Of the Jew it might be said more truly than of any other European people that the growth of population has led to overcrowding and has induced emigration. Yet of no people is this less true, for, were it not for the discrimination and persecution directed against them, the Jews would be the most prosperous and least overcrowded of the races of Europe.

The Finns.—Until the year 1901 Finland was the freest and best governed part of the Russian Empire. Wrested from Sweden in 1809, it became a grand duchy of the Czar, guaranteed self-government, and confirmed by coronation oath of each successor. It was the only section of the Russian Empire with a constitutional government in which the laws, taxes, and army were controlled by a legislature representing the people. Here alone in all his empire was the Czar compelled to ask the consent of parliament in order to enact laws. But these free institutions within the past seven years were by his decree abrogated. The Czar claimed the right to put into force such laws as he chose without discussion or acceptance by the Finnish diet. The Russian language took the place of Swedish and Finnish as the official medium, a severe censorship of the press was introduced, the Lutheran religion, devoutly adhered to, was subordinated to the "orthodox," the independent Finnish army was abolished and Finns were distributed throughout the armies of the empire, and a Russian governor with absolute powers was placed over all. Thus have 2,000,000 of the sturdiest specimens of humanity been suddenly reduced to the level of Asiatic despotism. They had managed by industry and thrift to extort a livelihood from a sterile soil, and had developed a school system with universal education, culminating in one of the noblest universities of Europe. Their peasants are healthy, intelligent, honest, and sober. In one year, 1900, their emigration increased from 6000 to 12,000, and it continues at 14,000, notwithstanding the repentance of the Czar and his restoration of their stolen rights. Compared with the population of the country, the present immigration from Finland is proportionately greater than that of any race except the Jews; and famine, adding its horrors to the loss of their liberties, has served to augment the army of exiles.

Slav   Jewish   Polack   Lithuanian
(From *The Home Missionary*)

Much dispute has arisen respecting the racial relations of the Finns. Their language is like that of the Magyars, an agglutinative tongue with tendencies towards inflections, but their physical structure allies them more nearly to the Teutons. Their Lutheran religion also separates them from other peoples of the Russian Empire. Their sober industriousness and high intelligence give them a place above that of their intolerant conquerors; and the futile attempts of the Slav to "Russify" them drove to America many of our most desirable immigrants.

The French Canadians.—When Canada was conquered by England in 1759, it contained a French population of 65,000. Without further immigration the number had increased in 1901 to 2,400,000, including 1,600,000 in Canada and 800,000 emigrants and their children in the United States. Scarcely another race has multiplied as rapidly, doubling every twenty-five years. The contrast with the same race in France, where population is actually declining, is most suggestive. French Canada is, as it were, a bit of mediæval France, picked out and preserved for the curious student of social evolution. No French revolution broke down its old institutions, and the English conquest changed little else than the oath of allegiance. Language, customs, laws, and property rights remained intact. The only state church in North America is the Roman Catholic Church of Quebec, with its great wealth, its control of education, and its right to levy tithes and other church dues. With a standard of living lower than that of the Irish or Italians, and a population increasing even more rapidly, the French from Canada for a time seemed destined to displace other races in the textile mills of New England. Yet they came only as sojourners, intending by the work of every member of the family to save enough money to return to Canada, purchase a farm, and live in relative affluence. Their migration began at the close of the Civil War, and during periods of prosperity they swarmed to the mill towns, while in periods of depression they returned to their Northern homes. Gradually an increasing proportion remained in "the States," and the number in 1900 was 395,000 born in Canada, and 436,000 children born on this side of the line.

The Portuguese.—A diminutive but interesting migration of recent years is that of the Portuguese, who come, not from Portugal, but from the Cape Verde and Azores Islands, near equatorial Africa. These islands are remarkably overpopulated, and the emigration, nearly 9000 souls in 1906, is a very large proportion of the total number of inhabitants. By two methods did they find their way to America. One was almost accidental, for it was the wreck of a Portuguese vessel on the New England coast that first directed their attention to that section. They have settled mainly at New Bedford, Massachusetts, where they follow the fisheries in the summer and enter the mills in the winter. The other method was solicitation, which took several thousand of them to Hawaii as contract laborers on the sugar plantations. Unlike the Oriental importations to these islands the Portuguese insisted that their families be imported, and then as soon as their contracts expired they left the planters to become small farmers, and are now the backbone of the coffee industry. They and their children are nearly half of the "Caucasian" element of 30,000. In Massachusetts they are of two distinct types, the whites from the Azores and the blacks from the Cape Verde Islands, the latter plainly a blend of Portuguese and Africans. Their standards of living are similar to those of the Italians, though they are distinguished by their cleanliness and the neatness of their homes.

Syrians and Armenians.—That the recruiting area of American immigration is extending eastward is no more clearly evident than in the recent migration of Syrians and Armenians. These peoples belong to the Christian races of Asiatic Turkey, whence they are escaping the oppressions of a government which deserves the name of organized robbery rather than government. Within the past thirty years many thousand Syrians of Mount Lebanon have emigrated to Egypt and other Mediterranean countries, to the dependencies of Great Britain and South America. Six thousand of them came to the United States in 1906. They belong mainly to the Greek Church or the Maronite branch of the Roman Catholic Church, and it is mainly American missionary effort that has diverted them to the United States. Unlike other immigrants, they come principally from the towns, and are traders and pedlers. Broadly speaking, says an agent of the Charity Organization Society of New York, "the well-intentioned efforts of the missionaries have been abused by their protégés.... It is these alleged proselytes who have contributed largely to bring into relief the intrinsically servile character of the Syrian, his ingratitude and mendacity, his prostitution of all ideals to the huckster level.... As a rule they affiliate themselves with some Protestant church or mission, abandoning such connections when no longer deemed necessary or profitable."

The Armenian migration began with the monstrous Kurdish atrocities of recent years, instigated and supported by the Turkish government. Armenians are a primitive branch of the Christian religion, and at an early date became separated from both the Greek and Roman churches. They are among the shrewdest of merchants, traders, and money-lenders of the Orient, and, like the Jews, are hated by the peasantry and persecuted by the government. Like the Jews also, religious persecution has united them to the number of five million in a racial type of remarkable purity and distinctness from the surrounding races.

Asiatic Immigration.—Utterly distinct from all other immigrants in the nineteenth century are the Chinese. Coming from a civilization already ancient when Europe was barbarian, the Chinaman complacently refuses to assimilate with Americans, and the latter reciprocate by denying him the right of citizenship. His residence is temporary, he comes without his family, and he accumulates what to him is a fortune for his declining years in China. The gold discoveries of California first attracted him, and the largest migration was 40,000 in 1882, the year when Congress prohibited further incoming. In 1906, 3015 Chinamen tried to get in, and 2732 were admitted, mainly as United States citizens, returning merchants and returning laborers. One-half of the 1448 admitted as "exempt" were believed by the immigration officials to have been coolies in disguise.

Within the past ten years the Japanese have taken his place, and 14,000 of his Mongolian cousins arrived in 1906.

The immigration of the Japanese has taken a peculiar turn owing to the annexation of Hawaii. While these islands were yet a kingdom in 1868 this immigration began, and in 1886 a treaty was concluded with Japan for the immigration of Japanese contract laborers for the benefit of the sugar planters. Many thousand were imported under this arrangement, and "the fear that the islands would be annexed to Japan was one of the prime factors in the demand for annexation to the United States." With annexation in 1900 contract labor was abolished, and the Japanese, freed from servitude, indulged in "an epidemic of strikes." The Japanese government retained paternal oversight of its laborers migrating to foreign lands, which is done through some thirty-four emigrant companies chartered by the government. Since opening up Korea for settlement Japan has granted but a limited number of passports to its citizens destined for the mainland of America, so that almost the entire immigration comes first to Honolulu through arrangements made between the emigrant companies and the planters. But the planters are not able to keep them on the island on account of the higher wages on the Pacific coast. Since the alien contract-labor law does not apply to immigrants from Hawaii, a *padroni* system has sprung up for importing Japanese from that island. As a result, the arrivals at Honolulu are equalled by the departures to the mainland, and Hawaii becomes the American side entrance for the Japanese. This evasion has been stopped by the law of February 20, 1906.

Hawaii also is showing another Asiatic race the opening to America. The growing independence of the Japanese led the planters to seek Koreans, since the Chinese exclusion law came into force with annexation. In this effort to break down Japanese solidarity some eight thousand Koreans have been mixed with them during the past five years, and these also have begun the transit to California.

Although the Chinese, Japanese, and Koreans are the familiar examples often cited of low standards of living, yet their wages in their native countries are higher than those of the South Italians and equal to those of the Slavs. They earn $4 or $5 a month and spend $2 or $3 for living. In Hawaii they get $18 to $20 a month, and on the Pacific coast $35 to $50.

In the past two or three years a tiny dripping of immigration has found its way from another vast empire of Asiatic population—India. Some two hundred are admitted each year. The populations of that land are growing discontented as they see Indians returned from Natal, where they earned $20 to $35 a month, while at home they get only $3 to $7 under a penal contract system. The American consul at Calcutta reports ten sturdy Punjab Mohammedans inquiring the way to America and telling of their friends at work on American dairy farms. In his judgment they are stronger and more intelligent than the Chinese coolies and are preferable for work on the Panama Canal. The self-governing British colonies have educational restrictions designed to prevent Asiatic immigration, whether of British subjects or aliens; other colonies have contract labor. The unrest of India therefore turns the native eyes towards America.

While America has been welcoming the eastward and backward races she has begun to lose her colonial stock and her Americanized Teutonic stock. These pioneer elements have kept in front of the westward movement, and now that the American frontier is gone they seek a new frontier in Canada. The Canadian government for several years has sought to fill its vast Western plains with Teutonic races and to discourage others. It has expended many thousand dollars for advertising and soliciting in the British Isles, and has maintained twenty to thirty immigration agents in our Western states. The opportunities of British Columbia are now well known, and the American farmers, with agricultural land rising enormously in value, sell out to the newcomer or the acclimated immigrant and betake themselves to double or treble the area for cultivation under the flag of England. They push onward by rail and by wagon, and the ingress of millions of immigrants is reflected in the egress of thousands of Americans.

Indigenous Races.—It is not enough that we have opened our gates to the millions of divergent races in Europe, Asia, and Africa; we have in these latter days admitted to our fold new types by another process—annexation.

The Hawaiians are the latest of these oversea races to be brought under our flag, although in the course of eighty years they have been brought under our people. Nowhere else in the world has been seen such finished effect on an aboriginal race of the paradoxes of Western civilization—Christianity, private property, and sexual disease. With a population of some 300,000 at the time of discovery they had dwindled by domestic wars and imported disease to 140,000 when the missionaries came in 1820, then to 70,000 in 1850 when private property began its hunt for cheap labor, and now they number but 30,000. A disease eliminating the unfit of a race protected by monogamy decimates this primitive people on a lower stage of morals. Missionaries from the most intellectual type of American Protestantism converted the diminishing nation to Christianity in fifty years. A soil and climate the most favorable in the world for sugar-cane inspired American planters and sons of missionaries to displace the unsteady Hawaiians with industrious coolies, and finally to overthrow the government they had undermined and then annex it to America. Although acquiring American citizenship and sharing equally the suffrage with Caucasians, the decreasing influence of the Hawaiians is further diminished by the territorial form of government.

The Spanish War added islands on opposite sides of the globe, with races resulting from diametrically opposite effects of three centuries of Spanish rule. From Porto Rico the aboriginal Carib had long disappeared under the slavery of his conquerors, and his place had been filled by the negro slave in sugar cultivation and by the Spaniard and other Europeans in coffee cultivation. To-day the negro and mulatto are two-fifths of the million population and the whites three-fifths. In the Philippine Islands the native races have survived under a theocratic protectorate and even their tribal and racial subdivisions have been preserved. Two-fifths of their population of 7,600,000 belong to the leading tribe, the Visayans, and one-fifth to another, the Tagalogs. Six other tribes complete the list of "civilized" or Christianized peoples, while 10 per cent remain pagan in the mountains and forests. Four-fifths of the population are illiterate, a proportion the same as in Porto Rico, compared with less than half of the negroes and only one-sixteenth of the whites in the United States.

CHAPTER V

INDUSTRY

In preceding chapters we have seen the conditions in their foreign homes which spurred the emigrants to seek America. We have seen religious persecution, race oppression, political revolution, militarism, taxation, famine, and poverty conspiring to press upon the unprivileged masses and to drive the more adventurous across the water. But it would be a mistake should we stop at that point and look upon the migration of these dissatisfied elements as only a voluntary movement to better their condition. In fact, had it been left to the initiative of the emigrants the flow of immigration to America could scarcely ever have reached one-half its actual dimensions. While various motives and inducements have always worked together, and it would be rash to assert dogmatically the relative weight of each, yet to one who has carefully noted all the circumstances it is scarcely an exaggeration to say that even more important than the initiative of immigrants have been the efforts of Americans and ship-owners to bring and attract them. Throughout our history these efforts have been inspired by one grand, effective motive,—that of making a profit upon the immigrants. The desire to get cheap labor, to take in passenger fares, and to sell land have probably brought more immigrants than the hard conditions of Europe, Asia, and Africa have sent. Induced immigration has been as potent as voluntary immigration. And it is to this mercenary motive that we owe our manifold variety of races, and especially our influx of backward races. One entire race, the negro, came solely for the profit of ship-owners and landowners. Working people of the colonial period were hoodwinked and kidnapped by shippers and speculators who reimbursed themselves by indenturing them to planters and farmers. The beginners of other races have come through similar but less coercive inducements, initiated, however, by the demand of those who held American property for speculation or investment. William Penn and his lessees, John Law, the Dutch East India Company, and many of the grantees of lands in the colonies, sent their agents through Western Europe and the British Isles with glowing advertisements, advanced transportation, and contracts for indentured service by way of reimbursement. In the nineteenth century new forms of induced migration appeared. Victims of the Irish famine were assisted to emigrate by local and general governments and by philanthropic societies, and both the Irish and the Germans, whose migration began towards the middle of the century, were, in a measure, exceptions to the general rule of induced immigration for profit. Several Western states created immigration bureaus which advertised their own advantages for intending immigrants, and Wisconsin, especially, in this way settled her lands with a wide variety of races. After the Civil War, induced migration entered upon a vigorous revival. The system of indenturing had long since disappeared, because legislatures and courts declined to recognize and enforce contracts for service. Consequently a new form of importation appeared under the direction of middlemen of the same nativity as that of the immigrant. Chinese coolies came under contract with the Six Companies, who advanced their expenses and looked to their own secret agents and tribunals to enforce repayment with profit. Japanese coolies, much later, came under contract with immigration companies chartered by the Japanese government. Italians were recruited by the *padroni*, and the bulk of the new Slav immigration from Southeastern Europe is in charge of their own countrymen acting as drummers and middlemen.

INDUSTRIAL RELATIONS OF IMMIGRANTS—1906

Race or People	Total, 100 Per Cent	Sexes Males	Sexes Females	Ages Under 14 years	Ages 14-45 years	Ages Over 45 years	Total, 100 Per Cent	Occupations Professional	Occupations Commercial	Occupations Skilled	Occupations Unskilled
African (black)	3,786	62.2	37.8	9.1	86.8	4.1	2,921	3.0	2.6	45.6	48.8
Armenian	1,895	75.	24.9	11.	84	3.	1,39	3.4	5.1	38.	53.0

		1		8	.3	9	0			5	
Bohemian and Moravian	12,958	57.3	42.8	20.7	73.9	5.4	7,985	1.3	1.2	43.6	53.9
Bulgarian, Servian, and Montenegrin	11,548	96.2	3.8	1.9	96.2	1.9	11,025	0.1	0.3	3.7	95.9
Chinese	1,485	94.1	5.9	4.5	81.5	14.0	1,261	6.9	66.0	1.5	25.6
Croatian and Slovenian	44,272	86.5	13.5	3.8	94.1	2.1	40,125	0.1	0.1	3.7	96.1
Cuban	5,591	67.4	32.6	17.2	73.2	9.6	2,842	10.3	19.1	55.9	14.7
Dalmatian, Bosnian, and Herzegovinian	4,568	95.1	4.9	1.7	96.3	2.0	4,373	0.1	0.3	7.7	91.9
Dutch and Flemish	9,735	67.0	33.0	17.6	76.4	6.0	5,849	5.2	7.9	30.1	56.8
East Indian	271	93.0	7.0	5.5	90.5	4.0	222	9.9	52.7	5.4	32.0
English	45,079	62.1	37.9	13.5	75.3	11.2	28,249	10.8	13.5	51.3	24.4
Finnish	14,136	67.4	32.6	7.1	90.8	2.1	11,959	0.4	0.3	7.2	92.1
French	10,379	57.1	42.9	8.6	81.7	9.7	6,823	16.5	12.9	31.3	39.3
German	86,813	59.2	40.8	15.1	78.6	6.3	55,095	4.3	6.7	29.7	59.3
Greek	23,127	96.3	3.7	3.1	95.9	1.0	21,615	0.5	2.6	9.4	87.5
Hebrew	153,748	52.1	47.9	28.3	66.3	5.4	76,605	1.4	5.6	66.7	26.3
Irish	40,959	50.9	49.1	4.6	90.9	4.5	35,387	1.7	2.9	15.1	80.3
Italian (North)	46,286	78.9	21.1	8.6	87.9	3.5	36,980	1.4	2.3	19.4	76.9
Italian (South)	240,528	79.4	20.6	11.1	84.3	4.6	190,105	0.4	1.3	16.0	82.3
Japanese	14,24	89.	10.4	1.0	97	1.	11,7	2.2	10.3	2.8	84.7

45

Races and Immigrants in America

		3	6		.1	9	97				
Korean	127	81.1	18.9	16.5	81.1	2.4	80	6.3	15.0	2.5	76.2
Lithuanian	14,257	66.1	33.9	8.9	89.5	1.6	11,568	0.2	0.2	9.2	90.4
Magyar	44,261	71.8	28.2	9.0	87.5	3.5	34,559	0.6	0.5	9.3	89.6
Mexican	141	66.0	34.0	14.9	74.5	10.6	65	23.1	35.4	24.6	16.9
Pacific Islander	13	76.9	23.1	7.7	76.9	15.4	9	33.3	0.0	66.7	0.0
Polish	95,835	69.3	30.7	9.3	88.5	2.2	77,437	0.2	0.2	7.7	91.9
Portuguese	8,729	58.4	41.6	20.9	70.7	8.4	5,815	0.5	1.1	4.8	93.6
Roumanian	11,425	92.5	7.5	2.0	94.0	4.0	10,759	0.2	0.2	2.5	97.1
Russian	5,814	81.7	18.3	10.0	86.8	3.2	4,591	3.2	2.4	10.8	83.6
Ruthenian	16,257	75.7	24.3	3.6	93.9	2.5	14,899	0.1		2.7	97.2
Scandinavian	58,141	62.1	37.9	9.1	86.4	4.5	47,352	1.8	1.6	23.5	73.1
Scotch	16,463	66.1	33.9	12.9	78.8	8.3	11,207	5.7	9.9	62.8	21.6
Slovak	38,221	69.6	30.4	8.9	88.4	2.7	29,817		0.1	4.9	95.0
Spanish	5,332	83.6	16.4	7.1	84.6	8.3	4,211	5.7	19.2	44.4	30.7
Spanish American	1,585	69.7	30.3	17.0	74.4	8.6	790	23.7	37.1	21.1	18.1
Syrian	5,824	70.4	29.6	15.2	80.9	3.9	4,023	1.1	11.1	19.9	67.9
Turkish	2,033	95.7	4.3	1.9	96.0	2.1	1,914	1.5	4.4	8.3	85.8
Welsh	2,367	7.1	29.9	12.5	78.2	9.3	1,639	4.9	6.7	62.4	26.0
West Indian (except Cuban)	1,476	58.9	41.1	14.8	76.1	9.1	900	7.6	15.0	49.4	28.0
Other Peoples	1,027	94.5	5.5	2.6	96.0	1.4	932	1.2	4.1	18.0	76.7
Total	1,100,735	69.5	30.5	12.4	83.0	4.6	815,275	1.8	3.1	21.7	73.4

These labor speculators have perfected a system of inducements and through billing as effective as that by which horse and cattle buyers in Kentucky or Iowa collect and forward their living freight to the markets of Europe. A Croatian of the earlier immigration, for example, sets up a saloon in South Chicago and becomes an employment bureau for his "greener" countrymen, and also ticket agent on commission for the steamship companies. His confederates are stationed along the entire route at connecting points, from the villages of Croatia to the saloon in Chicago. In Croatia they go among the laborers and picture to them the high wages and abundant work in America. They induce them to sell their little belongings and they furnish them with through tickets. They collect them in companies, give them a countersign, and send them on to their fellow-agent at Fiume, thence to Genoa or other port whence the American steerage vessel sails. In New York they are met by other confederates, whom they identify by their countersign, and again they are safely transferred and shipped to their destination. Here they are met by their enterprising countryman, lodged and fed, and within a day or two handed over to the foreman in a great steel plant, or to the "boss" of a construction gang on a railway, or to a contractor on a large public improvement. After they have earned and saved a little money they send for their friends, to whom the "boss" has promised jobs. Again their lodging-house countryman sells them the steamship ticket and arranges for the safe delivery of those for whom they have sent. In this way immigration is stimulated, and new races are induced to begin their American colonization. Eventually the pioneers send for their families, and it is estimated that nearly two-thirds of the immigrants in recent years have come on prepaid tickets or on money sent to them from America.

The significance of this new and highly perfected form of inducement will appear when we look back for a moment upon the legislation governing immigration.

Immigration Legislation.—At the close of the Civil War, with a vast territory newly opened to the West by the railroads, Congress enacted a law throwing wide open our doors to the immigrants of all lands. It gave new guaranties for the protection of naturalized citizens in renouncing allegiance to their native countries, declaring that "expatriation is a natural and inherent right of all people, indispensable to the enjoyment of the rights of life, liberty, and the pursuit of happiness."

In the same year, 1868, the famous Burlingame treaty was negotiated with China, by which Americans in China and Chinese in America should enjoy all the privileges, immunities, and exemptions enjoyed by citizens of the most favored nation. These steps favorable to immigration were in line with the long-continued policy of the country from the earliest colonial times.

But a new force had come into American politics—the wage-earner. From this time forth the old policies were violently challenged. High wages were to be pitted against high profits. The cheap labor which was eagerly sought by the corporations and large property owners was just as eagerly fought by the unpropertied wage-earners. Of course neither party conceded that it was selfishly seeking its own interest. Those who expected profits contended that cheap foreign labor was necessary for the development of the country; that American natural resources were unbounded, but American workmen could not be found for the rough work needed to turn these resources into wealth; that America should be in the future, as it had been in the past, a haven for the oppressed of all lands; and that in no better way could the principles of American democracy be spread to all peoples of the earth than by welcoming them and teaching them in our midst.

The wage-earners have not been so fortunate in their protestations of disinterestedness. They were compelled to admit that though they themselves had been immigrants or the children of immigrants, they were now denying to others what had been a blessing to them. Yet they were able to set forward one supreme argument which our race problems are every day more and more showing to be sound. The future of American democracy is the future of the American wage-earner. To have an enlightened and patriotic citizenship we must protect the wages and standard of living of those who constitute the bulk of the citizens. This argument had been offered by employers themselves when they were seeking a protective tariff against the importation of "pauper-made" goods. What wonder that the wage-earner should use the same argument to keep out the pauper himself, and especially that he should begin by applying the argument to those races which showed themselves unable rapidly to assimilate, and thereby make a stand for high wages and high standards of living. Certain it is that had the white wage-earners possessed the suffrage and political influence during colonial times, the negro would not have been admitted in large numbers, and we should have been spared that race problem which of all is the largest and most nearly insoluble.

For it must be observed in general that race antagonism occurs on the same competitive level. What appear often to be religious, political, and social animosities are economic at bottom, and the substance of the economic struggle is the advantage which third parties get when competitors hold each other down. The Southern planter was not hostile to the negro slave—he was his friend and protector. His nurse was the negro "mammy," his playmates were her children, and the mulatto throws light on his views of equality. It was the poor white who hated the negro and fled from his presence to the hills and the frontier, or sank below his level, despised by white and black. In times of freedom and reconstruction it is not the great landowner or employer that leads in the exhibition of race hostility, but the small farmer or wage-earner. The one derives a profit from the presence of the negro—the other loses his job or his farm. With the progress of white democracy in place of the old aristocracy, as seen in South Carolina, hostility to the negro may be expected to increase. With the elimination of the white laborer, as seen in the black counties, the relations of negro and planter are harmonious.

So it is in the North. The negro or immigrant strike breaker is befriended by the employer, but hated by the employee. The Chinaman or Japanese in Hawaii or California is praised and sought after by the employer and householder, but dreaded by the wage-earner and domestic. Investors and landowners see their properties rise in value by the competition of races, but the competitors see their wages and jobs diminish. The increase of wealth intensifies the difference and raises up professional classes to the standpoint of the capitalists. With both of them the privilege of leisure depends on the presence of servants, but the wage-earners do their own work. As the immigrant rises in the scale, the small farmer, contractor, or merchant feels his competition and begins to join in measures of race protection.

This hostility is not primarily racial in character. It is the competitive struggle for standards of living. It appears to be racial because for the most part races have different standards. But where different races agree on their standards the racial struggle ceases, and the negro, Italian, Slav, and American join together in the class struggle of a trade-union. On the other hand, if the same race has different standards, the economic struggle breaks down even the strongest affinities of race. The Russian Jew in the sweat-shop turns against the immigrant Jew, fleeing from the very persecution that he himself has escaped, and taking his place in the employment of the capitalist German Jew. It is an easy and patriotic matter for the lawyer, minister, professor, employer, or investor, placed above the arena of competition, to proclaim the equal right of all races to American opportunities; to avow his own willingness to give way should even a better Chinaman, Hindu, or Turk come in to take his place; and to rebuke the racial hatred of those who resist this displacement. His patriotism and world-wide brotherhood cost him and his family nothing, and indeed they add to his profits and leisure. Could he realize his industrial position, and picture in imagination that of his fellow-citizens, their attitude would not appear less disinterested than his own. The immigrant comes as a wage-earner, and the American wage-earner bears the initial cost of his Americanization. Before he acquired the suffrage his protest was unheard—after he gained political power he began to protect himself.

The first outbreak of the new-found strength of the American wage-earner was directed against a race superior even to the negro immigrants in industry, frugality, intelligence, and civilization—the Chinese. And this outbreak was so powerful that, in spite of all appeals to the traditions and liberties of America, the national government felt driven to repudiate the treaty so recently signed with the highest manifestations of faith, good-will, and international comity.

Very early in the settlement of California the Chinaman had encountered hostile legislation. The state election had been carried by the Knownothings as early as 1854. Discriminating taxes, ordinances, and laws were adopted, and even immigration was regulated by the state legislature. But the state and federal courts declared such legislation invalid as violating treaties or interfering with international relations. Then the wage-earning element of California joined as one man in demanding action by the federal government, and eventually, by the treaty of 1880 and the law of 1888, Chinese laborers were excluded. Thus did the Caucasian wage-earner score his first and signal victory in reversing what his opponents proclaimed were "principles coeval with the foundation of our government."

The next step was the Alien Contract Labor law of 1885 and 1888, placed on the statute books through the efforts of the Knights of Labor and the trades-unions. As early as 1875 Congress had prohibited the immigration of paupers, criminal, and immoral persons, but the law of 1885 went to the other extreme and was designed to exclude industrial classes. The law is directed against prepayment of transportation, assistance, or encouragement of foreigners to immigrate *under contract* to perform labor in the United States, and provides for the prosecution of the importer and deportation of the contract immigrant. This law has been enforced against skilled labor, which comes mainly from northwestern Europe, but, owing to the new system of *padroni* and middlemen above described, it cannot be enforced against the unskilled laborers of Southern and Eastern Europe, since it cannot be shown that they have come under contract to perform labor. By the amendment and revised law adopted in 1903, after considerable discussion, and an effort on the part of the labor unions to strengthen the law, it was extended so as to exclude not only those coming under contract but also those coming under *offers* and *promises* of employment.

From what precedes we see that there are two exactly opposite points of view from which the subject of immigration is approached. One is the production of wealth; the other is the distribution of wealth. He who takes the standpoint of production sees the enormous undeveloped resources of this country—the mines to be exploited, railroads and highways to be built and rebuilt, farms to be opened up or to be more intensively cultivated, manufactures to be multiplied, and the markets of the world to be conquered by our exports, while there are not enough workmen, or not enough willing to do the hard and disagreeable work at the bottom.

He who takes the standpoint of distribution sees the huge fortunes, the low wages, the small share of the product going to labor, the sweat-shop, the slums, all on account of the excessive competition of wage-earner against wage-earner.

Consider first the bearing of immigration on the production of wealth.

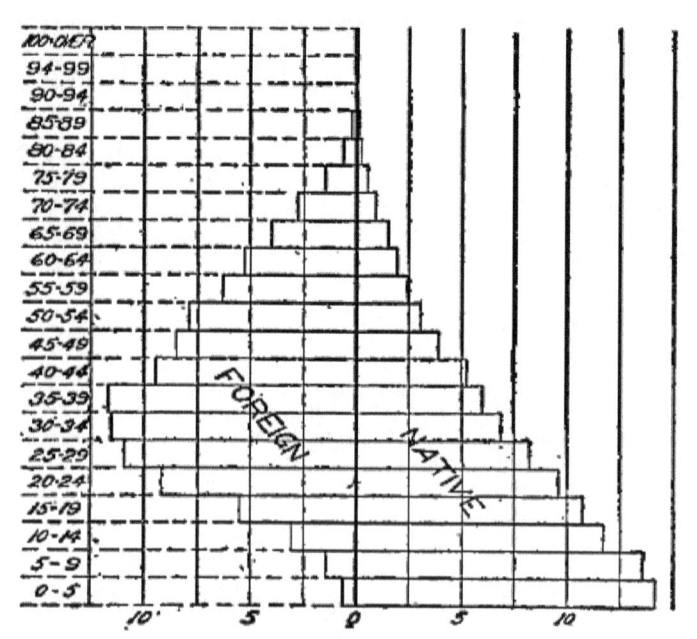

Age Groups, Foreign and Native-born

Immigration and Wealth Production.—Over four-fifths of the immigrants are in the prime of life—the ages between fourteen and forty-five. In the year 1906 only 12 out of every 100 were under fourteen years of age, and only 4.5 out of every 100 over forty-five years of age. The census of 1900 offers some interesting comparisons between the native-born and the foreign-born in this matter of age distribution. It shows quite plainly that a large proportion of the native-born population is below the age of industrial production, fully 39 per cent, or two-fifths, being under fifteen years of age, while only 5 per cent of the foreign-born are of corresponding ages. On the other hand, the ages fifteen to forty-four include 46 per cent of the native and 58 per cent of the foreign-born. This is shown in the diagram based on five-year age periods. The native born are seen to group themselves in a symmetrical pyramid, with the children under five as the wide foundation, gradually tapering to the ages of eighty and eighty-four, but for the foreign-born they show a double pyramid, tapering in both directions from the ages of thirty-five to thirty-nine, which include the largest five-year group. Thus, immigration brings to us a population of working ages unhampered by unproductive mouths to be fed, and, if we consider alone that which produces the wealth of this country and not that which consumes it, the immigrants add more to the country than does the same number of native of equal ability. Their home countries have borne the expense of rearing them up to the industrial period of their lives, and then America, without that heavy expense, reaps whatever profits there are on the investment.

1 - NATIVE
2 - FOREIGN > WHITE
3 - IMMIGRANTS 1906

	MALES	FEMALES	
1	50.7	49.3	1
2	54.0	46.0	2
3	69.4	30.6	3

Proportion of Sexes. Native and Foreign-born Whites, 1900, and Immigrants 1906

In another respect does immigration add to our industrial population more than would be done by an equal increase in native population, namely, by the large excess of men over women. In 1906, over two-thirds of the immigrants were males and less than one-third were females. This is shown on the accompanying diagram, as well as the fact based on the census statistics that among the foreign-born the men predominate over the women in the ratio of 540 to 460, while among the native-born population the sexes are about equal, being in the proportion of 507 males to 493 females.

This small proportion of women and children shows, of course, that it is the workers, not the families, who seek America. Yet the proportions widely vary for different nationalities. Among the Jews 48 per cent are females and 28 per cent children. This persecuted race moves in a body, expecting to make America its home. At the other extreme the Greeks send only 4 per cent females and 3 per cent children, the Croatians 13 per cent females and 4 per cent children, the South Italians 21 per cent females and 11 per cent children. These are races whose immigration has only recently begun, and naturally enough the women and children, except in the case of the Jews, do not accompany the workmen. A race of longer migration, like the Germans, has 41 per cent females and 15 per cent children. The Irish have a peculiar position. Alone of all the races do the women equal the men, but only 5 per cent are children. Irish girls seeking domestic service explain this preponderance of women. Significant and interesting facts regarding other races may be seen by studying the table entitled "Industrial Relations of Immigrants."

Sweden Greece Germany Russia China Scotland
Austria Australia Canada England Italy Roumania

American School Boys
(From *World's Work*)

Such being the proportions of industrial energy furnished by immigration, what is the quality? Much the larger proportion of immigrants are classed as unskilled, including laborers and servants. Omitting those who have "no occupation," including mainly women and children, who are 30.5 per cent of the total, only 21.7 per cent of the remainder who are working immigrants are skilled, and 73.4 per cent are unskilled. The proportions vary greatly among the different races. The largest element of skilled labor is among the Jews, a city people, two-thirds of whom are skilled workmen. Nearly the same proportion of the Scotch and Welsh and over one-half of the English and Bohemians are skilled mechanics. Nearly one-third of the Germans and Dutch are skilled, and one-fourth of the Scandinavians. At the other extreme, only 3 to 5 per cent of the Ruthenians, Croatians, Roumanians, and Slovaks are skilled, and 8 to 10 per cent of the Magyars, Lithuanians, and Poles. One-fifth of the North Italians and one-sixth of the South Italians are skilled. These and other proportions are shown in the statistical table.

The skilled labor which comes to America, especially from Northern and Western Europe, occupies a peculiar position in our industries. In the first place, the most capable workmen have permanent places at home, and it is, in general, only those who cannot command situations who seek their fortunes abroad. The exceptions to this rule are in the beginnings of an industry like that of tin plate, when a large proportion of the industry moved bodily to America, and the highly skilled tin workers of Wales brought a kind of industrial ability that had not hitherto existed in this country. As for the bulk of skilled immigrants, they do not represent the highest skill of the countries whence they come.

On the other hand, the European skilled workman is usually better trained than the American, and in many branches of industry, especially machinery and ship-building, the English and Scotch immigrants command those superior positions where an all-round training is required.

This peculiar situation is caused by the highly specialized character of American industry. In no country has division of labor and machinery been carried as far as here. By division of labor the skilled trades have been split up into simple operations, each of which in itself requires little or no skill, and the boy who starts in as a beginner is kept at one operation so that he does not learn a trade. The old-time journeyman tailor was a skilled mechanic who measured his customer, cut the cloth and trimmings, basted, sewed, and pressed the suit. Now we have factories which make only coats, others which make only vests, others trousers, and there are children's knee-pants factories and even ladies' tailor establishments where the former seamstress sees her precious skill dissipated among a score of unskilled workers. Thus the journeyman tailor is displaced by the factory, where the coat passes through the hands of thirty to fifty different men and women, each of whom can learn his peculiar operation in a month or two. The same is true in greater or less degree in all industries. Even in the building trades in the larger cities there are as many kinds of bricklayers as there are kinds of walls to be built, and as many kinds of carpenters as there are varieties of woodwork.

So it is with machinery. The American employer does not advertise for a "machinist"— he wants a "lathe hand" or a "drill-press hand," and the majority of his "hands" are perhaps only automatic machine tenders. The employer cannot afford to transfer these hands from one job to another to enable them to "learn the trade." He must keep them at one operation, for it is not so much skill that he wants as cheap labor and speed. Consequently, American industry is not producing all-round mechanics, and the employers look to Europe for their skilled artisans. In England the trade-unions have made it their special business to see that every apprentice learns every part of his trade, and they have prevented employers from splitting up the trades and specializing machinery and thereby transforming the mechanic into the "hand." Were it not for immigration, American industries would ere now have been compelled to give more attention to apprenticeship and the training of competent mechanics. The need of apprenticeship and trade schools is being more seriously felt every year, for, notwithstanding the progress of division of labor and machinery, the all-round mechanic continues to play an important part in the shop and factory. American trade-unions are gaining strength, and one of their most insistent demands is the protection of apprenticeship. The bricklayers' and carpenters' unions of Chicago even secure from their employers instruction for apprentices in school. Not much headway in this line, however, has yet been made, and American industry has become abnormal, we might almost say suicidal, or at any rate, non-self-supporting. By extreme division of labor and marvellous application of machinery it makes possible the wholesale employment in factories of the farm laborers of Europe and their children, and then depends on Europe for the better-trained types of the skilled mechanic, who, on account of the farm laborer, have not been able to learn their trade in America.

Not only does immigration bring to America the strongest, healthiest, and most energetic and adventurous of the work-people of Europe and Asia, but those who come work much harder than they did at home. Migration tears a man away from the traditions, the routine, the social props on which he has learned to rely, and throws him among strangers upon his own resources. He must swim or drown. At the same time he earns higher wages and eats more nourishing food than he had ever thought within reach of one in his station. His ambition is fired, he is stirred by the new tonic of feeling himself actually rising in the world. He pictures to himself a home of his own, he economizes and saves money to send to his friends and family, or to return to his beloved land a person of importance. Watch a gang of Italians shovelling dirt under an Irish boss, or a sweat-shop of Jewish tailors under a small contractor, and you shall see such feverish production of wealth as an American-born citizen would scarcely endure. Partly fear, partly hope, make the fresh immigrant the hardest, if not the most intelligent, worker in our industries.

Industrial Capacities of Different Races.—But, however hard one may work, he can only exercise the gifts with which nature has endowed him. Whether these gifts are contributed by race or by civilization, we shall inquire when we come to the problems of amalgamation and assimilation. At present we are concerned with the varying industrial gifts and capacities of the various races as they actually exist at the time when immigration, annexation, or conquest takes place.

The mental and moral qualities suited to make productive workers depend upon the character of the industry. It is not conceivable that the immigrants of the present day from Southern Europe and from Asia could have succeeded as frontiersmen and pioneers in the settlement of the country. In all Europe, Asia, and Africa there was but one race in the seventeenth and eighteenth centuries that had the preliminary training necessary to plunge into the wilderness, and in the face of the Indian to establish homes and agriculture. This was the English and the Scotch-Irish. The Spaniards and the French were pioneers and adventurers, but they established only trading stations. Accustomed to a paternal government they had not, as a people, the self-reliance and capacity for sustained exertion required to push forward as individuals, and to cut themselves off from the support of a government across the ocean. They shrank from the herculean task of clearing the forests, planting crops among the stumps, and living miles away from their neighbors. True, the pioneers had among their number several of German, French, and Dutch descent, but these belonged to the second and third generations descended from the immigrants and thrown from the time of childhood among their English-Scotch neighbors. The French trappers and explorers are famous, and have left their names on our map. But it was the English race that established itself in America, not because it was first to come, not because of its armies and navies, but because of its agriculture. Every farm newly carved out of the wilderness became a permanent foothold, and soon again sent out a continuous colony of sons and daughters to occupy the fertile land. Based on this self-reliant, democratic, industrial conquest of the new world the military conquest naturally, inevitably followed.

But at the present day the character of industry has entirely changed. The last quarter of the nineteenth century saw the vacant lands finally occupied and the tribe of frontiersmen coming to an end. Population now began to recoil upon the East and the cities. This afforded to manufactures and to the mining industries the surplus labor-market so necessary for the continuance of large establishments which to-day need thousands of workmen and to-morrow hundreds. Moreover, among the American-born workmen, as well as the English and Scotch, are not found that docility, obedience to orders, and patient toil which employers desire where hundreds and thousands are brought like an army under the direction of foremen, superintendents, and managers. Employers now turn for their labor supply to those eastern and southern sections of Europe which have not hitherto contributed to immigration. The first to draw upon these sources in large numbers were the anthracite coal operators of Pennsylvania. In these fields the English, Scotch, Welsh, and Irish miners, during and following the period of the Civil War, had effected an organization for the control of wages, and the outrages of a secret society known as the Molly Maguires gave occasion for the importation of new races unaccustomed to unionism, and incapable, on account of language, of coöperation with English-speaking miners. Once introduced in the mining industry, these races rapidly found their way into the unskilled parts of manufactures, into the service of railroads and large contractors. On the construction of the Erie Canal in 1898, of 16,000 workmen, 15,000 were unnaturalized Italians. The census of 1900 showed that while the foreign-born males were one-fourteenth of the laborers in agriculture, they were three-fourths of the tailors, more than one-half of the cabinet makers, nearly one-half of the miners and quarrymen, tannery workers, marble and stonecutters, more than two-fifths of the boot and shoe-makers and textile workers, one-third of the coopers, iron and steel workers, wood-workers and miscellaneous laborers, one-fourth of the carpenters, painters, and plasterers, and one-fifth of the sawmill workers. The foreign-born females numbered nearly two-fifths of the female cotton-mill operatives and tailors, one-third of the woollen-mill operatives, one-fourth of the tobacco and silk-mill operatives.

On the Pacific slope the Chinese and Japanese immigrants have filled the place occupied by the southeast European in the East and the negro in the South. They were the workmen who built the Pacific railroads, and without them it is said that these railroads could not have been constructed until several years after their actual completion.

The immigration of the Chinese reached its highest figures prior to the exclusion laws of 1882, and since that time has been but an insignificant contribution. In their place have come the Japanese, a race whose native land, in proportion to its cultivable area, is more densely populated than any other country in the world. The Chinese and Japanese are perhaps the most industrious of all races, while the Chinese are the most docile. The Japanese excel in imitativeness, but are not as reliable as the Chinese. Neither race, so far as their immigrant representatives are concerned, possesses the originality and ingenuity which characterize the competent American and British mechanic. In the Hawaiian Islands, where they have enjoyed greater opportunities than elsewhere, they are found to be capable workmen of the skilled trades, provided they are under the direction of white mechanics. But their largest field of work in Hawaii is in the unskilled cultivation of the great sugar plantations. Here they have been likened to "a sort of agricultural automaton," and it becomes possible to place them in large numbers under skilled direction, and thus to secure the best results from their docility and industry.

In the United States itself the plantation form of agriculture, as distinguished from the domestic form, has always been based on a supply of labor from backward or un-Americanized races. This fact has a bearing on the alleged tendency of agriculture toward large farms. Ten years ago it seemed that the great "bonanza" farms were destined to displace the small farms, just as the trust displaces the small manufacturer. But it is now recognized that the reverse movement is in progress, and that the small farmer can compete successfully with the great farmer. It has not, however, been pointed out that the question is not merely an economic one and that it depends upon the industrial character of the races engaged in agriculture. The thrifty, hard-working and intelligent American or Teutonic farmer is able to economize and purchase his own small farm and compete successfully with the large undertaking. He is even beginning to do this in Hawaii since the compulsory labor of his large competitors was abolished. But the backward, thriftless, and unintelligent races succeed best when employed in gangs on large estates. The cotton and sugar fields of the South with their negro workers have their counterpart in the plantations of Hawaii with their Chinese and Japanese, and in the newly developed sugar-beet fields of Nebraska, Colorado, and California, with their Russians, Bohemians, Japanese, and Mexicans. In the domestic or small form of agriculture the bulk of immigrants from Southern and Eastern Europe are not greatly desired as wage-earners, and they do not succeed as proprietors and tenants because they lack oversight and business ability. Where they are located in colonies under favorable auspices the Italians have achieved notable success, and in the course of Americanization they will doubtless rival older nationalities. But in the immigrant stage they are helpless, and it is the immigrants from Northwestern Europe, the Germans and Scandinavians, whose thrift, self-reliance, and intensive agriculture have made them from the start the model farmers of America.

The Jewish immigrant, particularly, is unfitted for the life of a pioneer. Remarkably individualistic in character, his field of enterprise is society, and not the land. Of the thirty thousand families sent out from New York by industrial and agricultural removal societies, nine-tenths are located in industry and trade, and the bulk of the remainder, who are placed on farms, succeed by keeping summer boarders. Depending on boarders, they neglect agriculture and buy their food-stuff. Their largest colony of hoped-for agriculturists, Woodbine, New Jersey, has become a clothing factory. Yet the factory system, with its discipline and regular hours, is distasteful to the Jew's individualism. He prefers the sweat-shop, with its going and coming. If possible, he rises through peddling and merchandising.

These are a few of the many illustrative facts which might be set forth to show that the changing character of immigration is made possible by the changing character of industry; and that races wholly incompetent as pioneers and independent proprietors are able to find a place when once manufactures, mines, and railroads have sprung into being, with their captains of industry to guide and supervise their semi-intelligent work.

CHAPTER VI

LABOR

We have seen that the character of the immigrants for whom a place can be found depends upon the character of the industry. It also depends upon the laws governing property in labor. Here the industrial problem widens out into the social problem.

There are four variations in the treatment of labor as property in the United States, each of which has had its peculiar effect on the character of immigration, or has grown out of the relations between races. They are slavery, peonage, contract labor, and free labor. Under slavery the laborer and his children are compelled by law throughout their lifetime to work for an owner on terms dictated and enforced by him. Under peonage the laborer is compelled by law to pay off a debt by means of his labor, and under contract labor he is compelled by law to carry out a contract to work. To enforce peonage and contract labor the offence of "running away" is made punishable by imprisonment at forced labor, or by extension of the period of service. Under freedom the law refuses to enforce a contract to work, making this an exception to the sacredness of contracts, and refuses to enforce the payment of a debt by specific service. This leaves to the contractor or creditor the usually empty relief of suing for damages. The significance of these varying degrees of servile, semi-servile, and free labor will be seen in the following discussion of the social relations of the superior and inferior races.

In the entire circuit of the globe those races which have developed under a tropical sun are found to be indolent and fickle. From the standpoint of survival of the fittest, such vices are virtues, for severe and continuous exertion under tropical conditions bring prostration and predisposition to disease. Therefore, if such races are to adopt that industrious life which is a second nature to races of the temperate zones, it is only through some form of compulsion. The negro could not possibly have found a place in American industry had he come as a free man, and at the present time contract labor and peonage with the crime of "running away" are recognized in varying degrees by the laws of Southern states. These statutes have been held unconstitutional by the Supreme Court, under an act of Congress passed in 1867, but the condition of peonage which they contemplate is considered by many planters as essential to the continuance of the cotton industry. One of them, in southwestern Georgia, a graduate of Columbia College, with five years of business training in the Northern states, is quoted in an interview as follows:—

"We have two ways of handling our plantations. We rent small sections of forty acres each, and with these go a plough and the mule. In addition, I have about 450 hands who work on wages. These men are paid nine dollars a month, in addition to a fixed rate of food, which amounts to four pounds of meat a week, a certain percentage of vegetables, tobacco, sugar, flour, and some other commodities.

"These negroes live on the plantation, are given a roof over their heads, have garden patches, and several other more or less valuable privileges. They invariably come to me for small advances of money.

"These advances of money and rations and clothing, although there is not much of the latter, are frequently sufficient to put the negro in debt to us. The minute he finds he is in debt he naturally conceives it to be easier to go to work somewhere else and begin all over again, instead of paying his debts.

"Now, when a negro runs away and violates his contract, leaving us in the lurch, not only short of his labor, but short of the advances we have made to him in money and goods, what would happen if we depended simply and solely on our right to sue? In the first place, with 450 hands we would have 450 suits before the season is out, and if we won them all we would not be able to collect forty-five cents.

"The result is, that in Georgia and Alabama, and I believe in other states, the law recognizes the right of the planter to reclaim the laborer who has left in violation of his contract, whether he be actually in debt or not.

"Whether Judge Jones has declared this law constitutional or not, the planters in the black belt will have to maintain their right to claim their contract labor, or else they will have to go out of the business. Under any other system you would find it impossible to get in your cotton, because the negroes at the critical time would simply sit down and refuse to work. When they are well, we compel laborers to go to the field by force. This is the truth, and there is no use lying about it."

This reasoning is entirely logical from the business standpoint. If production of wealth is the standard, contracts must be fulfilled and debts must be paid. Otherwise capital will not embark in business. But the reasoning does not stop with the negro. Once established, the practice spreads to other races. Instances are cited of white men held in peonage, negroes holding other negroes, and Italians forced to work in a phosphate mine. It is an easy matter to get working men in debt. Many thousand rural justices keeping no records of convictions, hundreds of constables with fees depending on convictions, scores of petty crimes with penalties not usually enforced, contractors and planters eager for labor at the convict's rating of 35 cents a day—neither the negro nor the poor white is safe. Immigrants avoid a country with such a record. Not only the dread of forced labor for themselves but the dread of competition with the low wages that the forced labor of others implies, keep the immigrants away from the South. The fame of peonage is spread among them before they leave their native land. The business that rests on coerced labor damages the whole community for its own temporary gain. The right to quit work is as sacred for the workman as the right to enforce contracts for the capitalist. It is just as necessary to get energetic labor as it is to get abundant capital to embark in business. By recognizing the right of workmen to violate contracts, the employer learns to content himself with contracts that will not hurt when violated. He learns to appeal to the workman's motive to industry by methods that are not coercive. Admitting that the bulk of what is said about the negro's fickleness is true, he nevertheless is indiscriminately maligned. The thousands that are unreliable furnish a cloak for suppressing the hundreds that are industrious. I have made comparisons of the pay-rolls of two gas works in Southern cities—the one employing negro stokers at 11 cents an hour, the other whites at 22 cents an hour, and both working 12 hours a day seven days a week. The negroes put in as many hours between pay-days as did the whites, and if they "laid off" after pay-day it is no more than any class of white workmen would do after two weeks of such exhausting work. The negro in Southern cities can scarcely hope to rise above 12 cents an hour, and white mechanics have a way of working with negro helpers at 10 cents an hour in order to lift their own wages to 20 cents an hour. White wage-earners and white employers in the South speak of the negroes' efforts to get higher wages in the same words and tones as employers in the North speak of white wage-earners who have organized unions and demanded more pay. A foreman condemned his "niggers" for instability when they were leaving him at 10 cents an hour for a railroad job at 12½ cents an hour. Praising the Italians in comparison with the negro, he could not think of paying 17½ cents an hour for pick-and-shovel work, which Italians were said to be getting in another section of the state. The right to quit work is the right to get higher wages. If the higher wages are paid and proper treatment accorded, a process of natural selection ensues. The industrious and steady workmen of all races retain the jobs. The gas company referred to above, by a system of graded pay advancing with years of service, had sorted out a more steady and reliable force of negroes than they could have secured of whites at the rate of wages paid. The test is indeed a severe one where a race has always been looked upon as servile. With high wages regarded as "white man's wages," the process of individual selection does not work out, and the dominant race excuses its resort to whipping, beating, and peonage on the ground of the laziness which its methods of remuneration have not learned to counterbalance. Even the industrious Italians treated in this way would not be industrious—they would leave for other states.

The Malay races, to which the Filipinos belong, are, like the negroes, careless, thriftless, and disinclined to continuous exertion. In order to induce the Javanese to work, the Dutch government of Java sets aside a certain tract of government land for coffee planting, and compels each head of a household to set out and keep in order a certain number of coffee trees. On private estates in Java and in other Malay and Indian colonies, such as Burma, Ceylon, British India, where the government does not compel the native to take a contract to work, it nevertheless enforces contracts voluntarily made. In certain provinces of the Philippines "the tenants are usually in debt, and the old law which permits the creditor to imprison the debtor for non-payment of debt is still in force.... Landowners of a district frequently come together shortly before the crops are sold and agree among themselves how much interest to charge the tenants on their debts. This is for the purpose of charging the highest possible rate and at the same time retain tenants, who then could not leave, finding the same conditions prevailing throughout the district." In densely populated countries like Java and Southern India, where the native cannot set up for himself, he has no alternative except to work under these contracts, and this is also true in the more thickly populated districts of the Philippine Islands. But the case is different in sparsely settled countries like Burma, East Sumatra, and the greater part of the Philippines, where wages are so high that natives are not compelled by necessity to work continuously. "Speaking generally," says Professor Jenks, "the unskilled Filipino laborer, while intelligent enough, is careless and thriftless. He in most cases wishes to take two or three days a week, on the average, to celebrate as feast days. In individual cases, where his wages have been increased, he has been known to lessen correspondingly the number of days per month which he would work. His income being sufficient to satisfy his modest needs, he could see no reason why he should toil longer than was necessary to earn his income."

Hence in these sparsely settled countries the Dutch and English governments have adopted, and Professor Jenks, in his report to the War Department, has recommended a limited use of the system of contract labor, not, however, for the native, but for imported Chinese. This system has existed in another of our newly acquired possessions, Hawaii, since 1852, where it applied to Chinese, Japanese, Portuguese, and German immigrants, and whence it was abolished by the act of annexation in 1898.

Filipino Governors
(From Census of the Philippine Islands)

Contract labor of this kind is quite different from the peonage and contract labor of the non-industrial races. It is similar to the indentured service of colonial times, in that the term of each contract is limited to a few years, and the contract is made by way of compensation for advanced expenses of immigration. The object is not, as in the case of slavery and peonage, to compel a shiftless race to work, but it is to develop the country by the introduction of an industrious race. The Chinese, after the expiration of their contracts, often become skilled laborers and merchants, and in the latter position their frugality and wiliness make them dangerous neighbors for the native Malay and Filipino races. For this reason Professor Jenks recommends that employers be placed under bonds to return each contract Chinese coolie to China at the expiration of the period of contract, not to exceed three years, unless the government gives special permission for renewal of the contract. Governor Taft, in his report for the year 1902, while advocating a limited employment of Chinese contract coolies, said, "the truth is that, from a political standpoint, the unlimited introduction of the Chinese into these islands would be a great mistake. I believe the objection on the part of the Filipinos to such a course to be entirely logical and justified. The development of the islands by Chinamen would be at the expense of the Filipino people, and they may very well resent such a suggestion."

Governor Taft's opinion is strongly supported by the special commissioner of the American Federation of Labor, who, after inquiries in the district surrounding Manila, reports as follows:—

"Their reluctance to work, continually harped upon by many employers, is simply the natural reluctance of a progressive people to work for low wages under bad treatment. When wages rise above the level of the barest and poorest necessaries of life, and where treatment is fair, there Filipinos are at work in any numbers required."

The situation here is similar to that of the negroes. In order to get two hundred steady workers at high wages it is necessary to try out a thousand or more. But the reports of the Philippine Commission show that with the process of selection which their engineers can pursue by means of the high wages on government work the results are satisfactory.

"Of course," continues Mr. Rosenberg in his report, "the Filipino worker cannot successfully compete—cheap as he can live—with the Chinese standard of living, hence the unceasing vilification of the Filipino workers by those employers and their following, who, seeing near by the unlimited supply of cheap Chinese labor, wish these islands to be thrown open to such labor, not only for the purpose of reducing the small wages of the Filipinos, but also to reduce that of the Chinese laborers now here. As one employer stated to me, 'We want more Chinese, to keep them here for one or two years, then ship them back and get another lot, for the Chinese I have here now are becoming too independent and want more pay.'"

Free Labor.—The free laborer is not compelled by law to work. Then why should he work? Why does he work? The answer is found within himself. He wants something that he cannot get without working. Though this may seem a trifling question and a self-evident answer, the question and answer are the foundation of all questions of free institutions. For the non-working races and classes or the spasmodic and unreliable workers are the savages, paupers, criminals, idiots, lunatics, drunkards, and the great tribe of exploiters, "grafters," despots, and "leisure classes," who live on the work of others. Nearly every question of social pathology may be resolved to this, Why does he not work? And nearly every social ill would be cured if the non-workers could be brought voluntarily to work.

There are just two grand motives which induce the freeman to work—necessity and ambition. Necessity is the desire for quantity, quality, and variety of things to be used. The term is elastic. It is psychological, not material. It includes, of course, the wants of mere animal existence—food, clothing, shelter. But this is a small part. The cost of the mere quantity needed to support life is less than the added cost needed to secure the quality and variety that satisfy the taste and habits. A pig enjoys raw corn, but a man requires corn cake at five times the cost. Tastes and habits depend on one's childhood, one's training, one's associations, and kind of work. The necessities of a Chinese coolie, Italian immigrant, or negro plantation hand are less, and cost less, than those of a skilled mechanic or a college graduate, because his associations have been different, and his present work is different. But necessity goes farther. It includes the wants of the family considered as a unit, and not merely the wants of the single man or woman, else the race would not continue to increase. Furthermore, social obligations impose added necessity. Compulsory education of children compels parents to support their children instead of living on their wages. Laws regulating sanitation and tenements compel the tenant to pay more rent. The necessities of a farm-hand on the estates of Italy are less than those of the same hand in the cities of America.

Ambition is the desire for an improved position for one's self and family—for better quality and greater variety of material things. It demands a style of clothing and living suitable to the improved position aspired to. It demands an education for one's children superior to the minimum set by compulsory schooling. It demands thrift and economy for the sake of independence or the ability to hold on until one's demands are conceded. Ambition looks to the future—necessity is based on the past. The negro or the Malay works three days and loafs three because three days' wages procure his necessities. The Chinaman, or Italian, or Jewish immigrant works six days and saves the wages of three because the future is vivid to his imagination. With similar necessities one is ambitious, the other is content.

The scope and possibility of evoking ambition depend upon the institution of private property. Property in human beings suppresses it, unless occasionally a slave is permitted to purchase his freedom. The wage system evokes ambition if the way is open for promotion or for escape by becoming an owner. Tenancy is on a still higher level, but most of all, for the masses of men, the ownership of his own small property is the keenest spur to ambition, for it rewards the worker with all of his product. This motive is the surest test of an individual's or a race's future. Compare the negro and the Italian cotton grower as tenants in the new vocation opening up to the latter. "It is always difficult," says the observant planter, Mr. Stone, "to get a negro to plant and properly cultivate the outer edges of his field—the extreme ends of his rows, his ditch banks, etc. The Italian is so jealous of the use of every foot for which he pays rent that he will cultivate with a hoe places too small to be worked with a plough, and derive a revenue from spots to which a negro would not give a moment's thought. I have seen them cultivate right down to the water's edge the banks of bayous that had never been touched by the plough. I have seen them walk through their fields and search out every skipped place in every row and carefully put in seed to secure a perfect stand. I have seen them make more cotton per acre than the negro on the adjoining cut, gather it from two to four weeks earlier, and then put in the extra time earning money by picking in the negro's field."

But ambition has its penalty. It is equivalent to an increase in the supply of labor. As an ambitious proprietor the increase goes into his permanent property, but the ambitious wage-earner accepts a lower rate of pay. His fellows see the reduction and go still lower. The see-saw continues until wages reach the level of necessities, and there is nothing left for ambition. The Jewish sweat-shop is the tragic penalty paid by that ambitious race. In the Illinois coal mines the wages were reduced one-third during twelve years of Italian and Slav immigration. The ambitious races are the industrial races. But their ambition and their industry bring the momentous problem of destructive competition. It might seem that this evil would correct itself—that an increase in the products of one industry would be offset by an increase in other industries; that therefore the increased supply in one would not be forced upon the market at lower prices, but would be exchanged on the same terms as before for the increased supply in others. This is indeed the case in prosperous times. All industries advance together, and the increasing supply of one is merely an increasing demand for others. But for some reason, industries do not always harmoniously advance together. And when the disproportion appears, the workers who are blindly but ambitiously pushing ahead endeavor to overcome, by increasing the quantity of output, what they lose by reducing the price. There is but one immediate and practical remedy—the organization of labor to regulate competition. The method of organization is to do in concert through self-sacrifice what the non-industrial races do individually for self-indulgence; namely, refuse to work. Where the one loafs the other strikes. While the necessities of the workers set the minimum below which wages cannot fall, and their physical endurance sets the maximum hours beyond which they cannot work, the labor-union, by means of the strike or the threat to strike, sets a higher minimum of wages and a lower maximum of hours, which leaves room for ambition. Eventually the higher wage and the shorter hours become habitual and become a higher level of necessities. Gifted individuals may, indeed, rise above the wage-earning class by their own efforts, but labor organization alone can raise the class as a whole.

The organization of workmen in labor unions has been more difficult in this than in other free countries, owing to the competition of races. Heretofore it has been the easiest possible matter for a manager, apprehensive of agitators in forming a union, to introduce a new race and a new language into his works. Indeed, almost the only device and symptom of originality displayed by American employers in disciplining their labor force has been that of playing one race against another. They have, as a rule, been weak in methods of conciliation and feelings of consideration for their employees, as well as in the means of safeguarding life and health, but they have been strong with the weapon "divide and conquer." The number of races they have drawn upon is often amazing. The anthracite mine workers comprise nineteen languages and dialects. The employees of the Colorado Fuel and Iron Company belong to thirty-two nationalities and speak twenty-seven languages. Such a medley of races offers indeed a disheartening prospect to the union organizer. And therefore when these races finally organize, the change in their moral character must be looked upon as the most significant of the social and industrial revolutions of our time. The United Mine Workers of America, with 300,000 members, is very largely composed of recent immigrants from Southern and Eastern Europe. So with the Longshoremen, the United Garment Workers, and the Butcher Workmen. These are or have been among the strongest and best disciplined of American labor-unions. The newest races of the past twenty years have been coming long enough to have members who speak the English language and act as interpreters and leaders, and this is essential where the speeches at a union meeting must be translated often into four or five languages before the subject can be voted upon. Furthermore, the recruiting area for new races has been nearly exhausted, and the races now coming find their fellow-countrymen already in the unions. In the anthracite coal field I saw a dozen Slovaks just arrived from Hungary, but persuaded by their unionized precursors not to take the places of strikers. In New York a shipload of Italians in time of strike has been taken directly into the union. Such a sight would have been unlikely a dozen years ago.

The competition of races is the competition of standards of living. The reason the Chinaman or the Italian can save three days' wages is because wages have been previously fixed by the greater necessities of more advanced races. But competition has no respect for superior races. The race with lowest necessities displaces others. The cotton textile industry of New England was originally operated by the educated sons and daughters of American stock. The Irish displaced many of them, then the French Canadians completed the displacement; then, when the children of the French had begun to acquire a higher standard, contingents of Portuguese, Greeks, Syrians, Poles, and Italians entered to prevent a rise, and latterly the Scotch-Irish from the Appalachian Mountains came down to the valleys of the South, and with their low wages, long hours, and child labor, set another brake on the standard of living. Lastly, Italians are beginning to be imported to supplement the "poor whites." Branches of the clothing industry in New York began with English and Scotch tailors, were then captured by Irish and Germans, then by Russian Jews, and lastly by Italians, while in Boston the Portuguese took a share, and in Chicago the Poles, Bohemians, and Scandinavians. Almost every great manufacturing and mining industry has experienced a similar substitution of races. As rapidly as a race rises in the scale of living, and through organization begins to demand higher wages and resist the pressure of long hours and overexertion, the employers substitute another race and the process is repeated. Each race comes from a country lower in the scale than that of the preceding, until finally the ends of the earth have been ransacked in the search for low standards of living combined with patient industriousness. Europe has been exhausted, Asia has been drawn upon, and there remain but three regions of the temperate zones from which a still lower standard can be expected. These are China, Japan, and India. The Chinese have been excluded by law, the Japanese and Koreans are coming in increasing numbers, and the Indian coolies remain to be experimented upon. That employers will make strenuous efforts to bring in these last remaining races in the progressive decline of standards, to repeal the Chinese prohibitive laws and to prevent additions to these laws, naturally follows from the progress toward higher standards and labor organization already made by the Italian and the Slav.

The trade-union is often represented as an imported and un-American institution. It is true that in some unions the main strength is in the English workmen. But the majority of unionists are immigrants and children of immigrants from countries that know little of unionism. Ireland and Italy have nothing to compare with the trade-union movement of England, but the Irish are the most effective organizers of the American unions, and the Italians are becoming the most ardent unionists. Most remarkable of all, the individualistic Jew from Russia, contrary to his race instinct, is joining the unions. The American unions, in fact, grow out of American conditions, and are an American product. Although wages are two or three times as high as in his European home, the immigrant is driven by competition and the pressure of employers into a physical exertion which compels him to raise his standard of living in order to have strength to keep at work. He finds also that the law forbids his children to work, and compels him to send them to school to maintain a higher standard and to support his children he must earn more wages. This he can do in no other way than by organizing a union. The movement is of course aided by English-speaking outsiders or "agitators," especially by the Irish, but it finds a prompt response in the necessities of the recruits. Labor organization is essentially the outcome of American freedom, both as a corrective to the evils of free competition and as an exercise of the privilege of free association.

When once moved by the spirit of unionism, the immigrants from low-standard countries are the most dangerous and determined of unionists. They have no obligations, little property, and but meagre necessities that compel them to yield. The bituminous coal miners were on strike four months in 1897 and the anthracite mine workers five months in 1902. Unionism comes to them as a discovery and a revelation. Suddenly to find that men of other races whom they have hated are really brothers, and that their enmity has been encouraged for the profit of a common oppressor, is the most profound awakening of which they are capable. Their resentment toward employers who have kept them apart, their devotion to their new-found brothers, are terrible and pathetic. With their emotional temperament, unionism becomes not merely a fight for wages but a religious crusade. It is in the nature of retribution that, after bringing to this country all the industrial races of Europe and Asia in the effort to break down labor organizations, these races should so soon have wiped out race antagonism and, joining together in the most powerful of labor-unions, have wrenched from their employers the greatest advances in wages.

There is but one thing that stands in the way of complete unionization in many of the industries; namely, a flood of immigration too great for assimilation. With nearly a million immigrants a year the pressure upon unions seems almost resistless. A few of the unions which control the trade, like the mine workers and longshoremen, with high initiation fees and severe terms of admission, are able to protect themselves by virtue of strength already gained. But in the coast states and on miscellaneous labor this strategic advantage does not exist, and the standards are set by the newest immigrants.

Governor Johnson of Minnesota.—Swede
(From *The World To-Day*)

Profits and Wages.—We have now stated at some length in this and the preceding chapter the two standpoints from which the immigration of industrial races is viewed. One standpoint is that of the production of wealth, the other the distribution of wealth. One is the development of our natural resources, the other is the elevation of our working population. If we inquire somewhat more critically and take into account all of the circumstances, we shall find that the motives animating this difference of policy are not really the above distinction between production and distribution, but the distinction between two opposing interests in distribution; namely, profits and wages. Unfortunately it is too readily assumed that whatever increases profits does so by increasing production. As a matter of fact it is only secondarily the production of wealth and development of resources that is sought by one of the interests concerned—it is primarily increase of profits at the expense of wages. Cheap labor, it is asserted, is needed to develop the less productive resources of the country—what the economists call the margin of production. It is needed to develop the less productive industries, like sugar beet, and the less productive branches of other industries, like the construction of railways in undeveloped regions or the reconstruction of railways in older regions, or the extension of a coal mine into the narrow veins, and so on. Without cheap labor these marginal resources, it is asserted, could not profitably be exploited, and would therefore not be developed.

This argument, within limits, is undoubtedly true, but it overlooks the part played by machinery and inventions where wages are high. The cigar-making machine cannot extensively be introduced on the Pacific coast because Chinese cheap labor makes the same cigars at less cost than the machines. High wages stimulate the invention and use of machinery and scientific processes, and it is machinery and science, more than mere hand labor, on which reliance must be placed to develop the natural resources of a country.

But machinery and science cannot be as quickly introduced as cheap immigrant labor. Machinery requires accumulation of capital in advance of production, but labor requires only the payment of daily wages in the course of production. Consequently in the haste to get profits the immigrant is more desired than machinery. But excessive profits secured in this way bring reaction and a period of business depression which check the production of wealth even more than the period of prosperity has stimulated production. Consider the extreme vacillations of prosperity and depression which characterize American industry. In a period of prosperity the prices of commodities rise rapidly, but the wages of labor, especially unorganized labor, follow slowly, and do not rise proportionately as high as prices. This means an enormous increase in profits and production of commodities. But commodities are produced to be sold, and if the market falls off, then production comes to a standstill with what is known as "overproduction." Now, wage-earners are the mass of consumers. If their wages do not rise in proportion to prices and profits, they cannot purchase as large a proportion of the country's products as they did before the period of prosperity began. "Overproduction" is mainly the "underconsumption" of wage-earners. Immigration intensifies this fatal cycle of "booms" and "depressions." A natural increase in population by excess of births over deaths, continues at practically the same rate year after year, in good times and bad times, but an artificial increase through immigration falls off in hard times and becomes excessive in good times. Thus, in 1879, at the lowest point of depression, the number of immigrants was 177,826, but three years later, in the "boom" culminating in 1882, it rose to 788,992. In nine years following the depression of 1897 the number increased from 230,000 to 1,100,000.

Even this does not tell the story complete, for the effects of free immigration are intensified by the opposite policy of a protective tariff on imports. While labor is admitted practically free, the products of labor are taxed to prevent free ingress. The following table shows the extreme points in the rise and fall of immigration and imports:—

CULMINATING POINTS OF IMMIGRATION AND IMPORTS OF MERCHANDISE

Year Ending June 30	Immigration Prosperity	Immigration Depression	Imports Prosperity	Imports Depression
1873	459,803		$642,000,000	
1879 and 1878		177,826		$437,000,000
1882	788,992		725,000,000	
1886 and 1885		334,203		578,000,000
1893	439,307		866,000,000	

1897 and 1898	230,832	616,000,000
1906	1,100,735	1,226,000,000

By comparing the two sets of columns it will be seen that, owing to the protective tariff, the imports of merchandise vary but slightly in periods of prosperity and depression compared with the variation in number of immigrants. Thus in the recent period of prosperity, the imports increased twofold above the lowest point of the preceding depression, while the number of immigrants increased nearly fivefold.

The swell of immigration in the above-mentioned periods of prosperity increases the supply of labor, but the protective tariff prevents a similar increase in the supply of products. Thus immigration and the tariff together prevent wages from rising with the rise in prices of commodities and cost of living. This permits profits to increase more than wages, to be followed by overproduction and stoppage of business.

Furthermore, when once the flow of immigrants is stimulated it continues for some time after the pinnacle of prosperity has been reached. In 1903 the boom met a check at the beginning of the year, but the number of immigrants continued to increase during the summer and fall at the rate of 20,000 per month in excess of the number during the high period of prosperity in 1902. This makes it possible for great corporations to continue their investments by means of cheap labor beyond the probable demands of the country, with the result of overproduction, loss of profits, inability to pay fixed charges, and consequent panics. Thus it is that immigration, instead of increasing the production of wealth by a steady, healthful growth, joins with other causes to stimulate the feverish overproduction, with its inevitable collapse, that has characterized the industry of America more than that of any other country. It helps to create fortunes during a period of speculation, and intensifies the reaction during a period of stagnation.

CHAPTER VII

CITY LIFE, CRIME, AND POVERTY

Statistics are considered by many people as dry and uninteresting, and the fact that a book is statistical is a warning that it should not be read, or that the statistical paragraphs should be passed over for the narrative and historical parts. This is a dilettante and lazy attitude to take, and especially so in the study of social subjects, for in these subjects it is only statistics that tell us the true proportions and relative importance of our facts. The study of statistics leads us to a study of social causes and forces, and when we see that in the year 1790 three per cent of our population lived in cities, and in the year 1900 thirty-three per cent lived in cities of 8000 population and over, we are aroused to the importance of making a serious inquiry into the reasons for this growth of cities and the effects of city life on the future of democracy and the welfare of the nation. More impressive to the student of race problems becomes the inquiry when we realize that while one-fifth of our entire population lives in the thirty-eight cities of over 100,000 population, two-fifths of our foreign-born population, one-third of our native offspring of foreign parents, and only one-tenth of our people of native parentage live in such cities. That is to say, the proportion of the foreign-born in great cities is four times as great, and the proportion of the children of foreign parents is three and one-third times as great as that of the colonial and older native stock. These proportions appear in the accompanying table and the upper diagram on page 162.

POPULATION IN THE UNITED STATES AND LARGE CITIES: 1900

Total for United States	In United States Number	Per cent	In 38 Cities of 100,000 Population and Over Number	Per cent of total of corresponding class
Population	75,994,575	100.0	14,208,347	18.7
Native white, native parents	40,958,216	53.9	4,245,817	10.3
Native white, foreign parents	15,637,063	20.6	5,280,186	33.2
Foreign white	10,213,817	13.4	3,972,324	39.7
Negroes	8,833,994	11.6	668,324	7.6
Indian and Mongolians	351,385	.5	32,696	9.3

If we present the matter in another form in order to show the full extent of foreign influence in our great cities, we have another diagram, which shows that 59 per cent of the population outside, and only 30 per cent of the population within these cities is of native parentage, while 27 per cent of the population outside, and 65 per cent of the population within these cities is of foreign parentage. The census enumeration carries us back only to the parents, but if we had knowledge of the grandparents we should probably find that the immigrant element of the nineteenth century contributed a goodly portion of those set down as of native parentage.

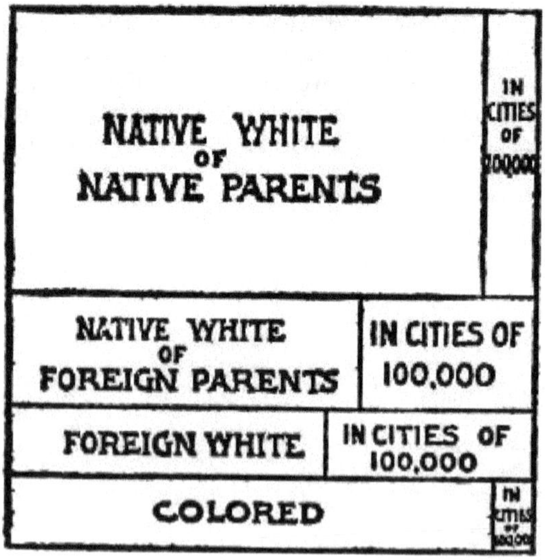
IN CITIES OF 100,000
NATIVE WHITE OF NATIVE PARENTS
NATIVE WHITE OF FOREIGN PARENTS
IN CITIES OF 100,000
FOREIGN WHITE
IN CITIES OF 100,000
COLORED

Distribution of Population: 1900

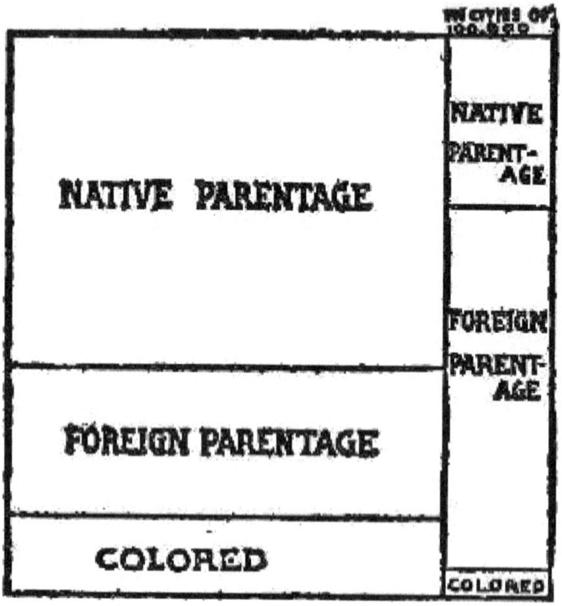
NATIVE PARENTAGE
NATIVE PARENT-AGE
FOREIGN PARENTAGE
FOREIGN PARENT-AGE
COLORED
COLORED

Percentage of Population in Cities: 1900

CONSTITUENTS OF THE POPULATION OF CITIES OF MORE THAN 100,000 INHABITANTS: 1900

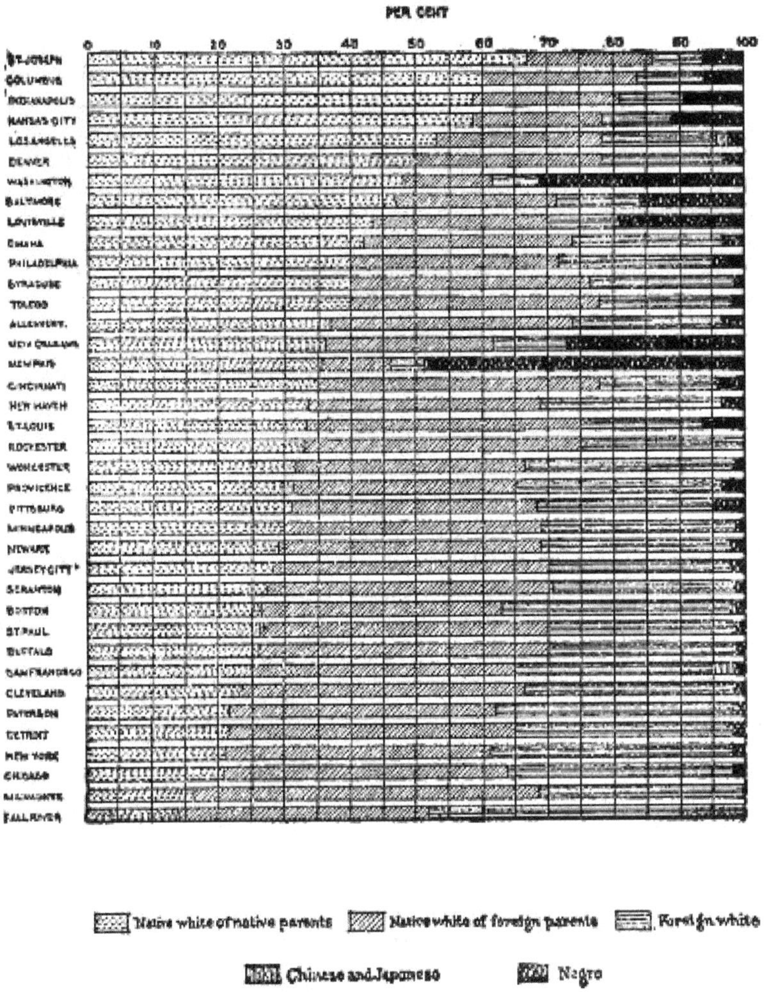

[Chart: bar chart showing composition of population by city, with categories: Native white of native parents, Native white of foreign parents, Foreign white, Chinese and Japanese, Negro]

Larger Image

Still more significant becomes the comparison when we take each of these cities separately, as is done in the chart reproduced on page 163 from the Statistical Atlas of the Twelfth Census.

Here it appears that the extreme is reached in the textile manufacturing city of Fall River, where but 14 per cent of the population is of native extraction, while in the two greatest cities, New York and Chicago, the proportion is 21 per cent, and the only large cities with a predominance of the native element are St. Joseph, Columbus, Indianapolis, and Kansas City, with Denver equally divided. As already stated, grandparents would still further diminish the proportion of native element.

If we carry our comparison down to the 160 cities of 25,000 population, we shall find that in such cities is one-half of the foreign-born population, and we shall also see marked differences among the races. At one extreme, three-fourths of those born in Russia, mainly Jews, live in these principal cities, and at the other extreme, one-fifth of the Norwegians.

The other Scandinavian countries and the Welsh and Swiss have about one-third, while the English and Scotch are two-fifths, Germany, Austria, Bohemia, and Poland, one-half to three-fifths, Ireland and Italy nearly two-thirds.

Individual cities suggest striking comparisons. In New York, computations based on the census show 785,035 persons of German descent, a number nearly equal to the population of Hamburg, and larger than the native element in New York (737,477). New York has twice as many Irish (710,510) as Dublin, two and one-half times as many Jews as Warsaw, half as many Italians as Naples, and 50,000 to 150,000 first and second generations from Scotland, Hungary, Poland, Austria, and England. Chicago has nearly as many Germans as Dresden, one-third as many Bohemians as Prague, one-half as many Irish as Belfast, one-half as many Scandinavians as Stockholm.

The variety of races, too, is astonishing. New York excels Babel. A newspaper writer finds in that city sixty-six languages spoken, forty-nine newspapers published in foreign languages, and one school at Mulberry Bend with children of twenty-nine nationalities. Several of the smaller groups live in colonies, like the Syrians, Greeks, and Chinese. But the colonies of the larger groups are reservoirs perpetually filling and flowing.

The influx of population to our cities, the most characteristic and significant movement of the present generation, has additional significance when we classify it according to the motives of those who seek the cities, whether industrial or parasitic. The transformation from agriculture to manufactures and transportation has designated city occupations as the opportunities for quick and speculative accumulation of wealth, and in the cities the energetic, ambitious, and educated classes congregate. From the farms of the American stock the sons leave a humdrum existence for the uncertain but magnificent rewards of industrialism. These become the business men, the heads of great enterprises, and the millionaires whose example hypnotizes the imagination of the farm lads throughout the land. Many of them find their level in clerical and professional occupations, but they escape the manual toil which to them is the token of subordination. These manual portions are the peculiar province of the foreign immigrant, and foreign immigration is mainly a movement from the farms of Europe to the cities of America. The high wages of the industries and occupations which radiate from American cities are to them the magnet which fortune-seeking is to the American-born. The cities, too, furnish that choice of employers and that easy reliance on charitable and friendly assistance which is so necessary to the indigent laborer looking for work. Thus it is that those races of immigrants the least self-reliant or forehanded, like the Irish and the Italians, seek the cities in greater proportions than those sturdy races like the Scandinavians, English, Scotch, and Germans. The Jew, also, coming from the cities of Europe, seeks American cities by the very reason of his racial distaste for agriculture, and he finds there in his coreligionists the necessary assistance for a beginning in American livelihood.

At this point we gradually pass over from the industrial motives of city influx to the parasitic motives. The United Hebrew Charities of New York have asserted that one-fourth of the Jews of that city are applicants for charity, and the other charitable societies make similar estimates for the population at large. These estimates must certainly be exaggerated, and a careful analysis of their methods of keeping statistics will surely moderate such startling statements, but we must accept them as the judgment of those who have the best means of knowing the conditions of poverty and pauperism in the metropolis. However exaggerated, they indicate an alarming extent of abject penury brought on by immigration, for it is mainly the immigrant and the children of the immigrant who swell the ranks of this indigent element in our great cities.

Those who are poverty-stricken are not necessarily parasitic, but they occupy that intermediate stage between the industrial and the parasitic classes from which either of these classes may be recruited. If through continued poverty they become truly parasitic, then they pass over to the ranks of the criminal, the pauper, the vicious, the indolent, and the vagrant, who, like the industrial class, seek the cities.

The dangerous effects of city life on immigrants and the children of immigrants cannot be too strongly emphasized. This country can absorb millions of all races from Europe and can raise them and their descendants to relatively high standards of American citizenship in so far as it can find places for them on the farms. "The land has been our great solvent." But the cities of this country not only do not raise the immigrants to the same degree of independence, but are themselves dragged down by the parasitic and dependent conditions which they foster among the immigrant element.

Dr. Oronhyatekha
Mohawk Indian, Late Chief of Order of Foresters

Crime.—This fact is substantiated by a study of criminal and pauper statistics. Great caution is needed in this line of inquiry, especially since the eleventh census in 1890 promulgated most erroneous inferences from the statistics compiled under its direction. It was contended by the census authorities that for each million of the foreign-born population there were 1768 prisoners, while for each million of the native-born there were only 898 prisoners, thus showing a tendency to criminality of the foreign-born twice as great as that of the white native-born. This inference was possible through oversight of the important fact that prisoners are recruited mainly from adults, and that the proportion of foreign-born adults to the foreign-born population is much greater than that of the native-born adults to the native population. If comparison be made of the number of male prisoners with the number of males of voting age, the proportions are materially different and more accurate, as follows:—

Number of Male Prisoners per Million of Voting Population, 1890 (Omitting "Unknown")

Native white, native parents	3,395
Native white, foreign parents	5,886
Native white, total	3,482
Foreign white	3,270
Negro	13,219

Here the foreign-born show actually a lower rate of criminality (3270) than the total native-born (3482). This inference harmonizes with our general observations of the immigrants, namely, that they belong to the industrial classes, and that our immigration laws are designed to exclude criminals.

But this analysis brings out a fact far more significant than any yet adverted to; namely, that the native-born children of immigrants show a proportion of criminality (5886 per million) much greater than that of the foreign-born themselves (3270 per million), and 70 per cent greater than that of the children of native parents.

This significant fact is further brought out, and with it the obverse of the census mistake above referred to, when we examine the census inferences respecting juvenile criminals. The census calculations show that there are 250 juvenile offenders for every million of the native-born population, and only 159 such offenders for every million of the foreign-born population; but if we remember that the proportion of foreign-born children is small, and then proceed to compare the number of boys who are offenders with the number of boys 10 to 19 years of age rather than with the number of persons of all ages, we shall have the following results, confining our attention to the North Atlantic states, where juvenile reformatories are more liberally provided than in other sections:—

Male Juvenile Offenders per Million of Male Population Ten To Nineteen Years of Age, North Atlantic States, 1890 (Omitting "Unknown")

Native white, native parents	1,744
Native white, foreign parents	3,923
Foreign white	3,316
Colored	17,915

This table throws a different light on the situation, for it shows that the tendency towards crime among juveniles, instead of being less for the foreign-born than for the native-born, is nearly twice as great as that of the children of American parentage, and that the tendency among native children of foreign parentage (3923 per million) is more than twice as great as that among children of American parents (1744 per million).

This amazing criminality of the children of immigrants is almost wholly a product of city life, and it follows directly upon the incapacity of immigrant parents to control their children under city conditions. The boys, especially, at an early age lose respect for their parents, who cannot talk the language of the community, and who are ignorant and helpless in the whirl of the struggle for existence, and are shut up during the daytime in shops and factories. On the streets and alleys, in their gangs and in the schools, the children evade parental discipline, and for them the home is practically non-existent. Says a well-informed student of race problems in New York, "Example after example might be given of tenement-house families in which the parents—industrious peasant laborers—have found themselves disgraced by idle and vicious grown sons and daughters. Cases taken from the records of charitable societies almost at random show these facts again and again." Even the Russian Jew, more devoted and self-sacrificing in the training of his children than any other race of immigrants, sees them soon earning more money than their parents and breaking away from the discipline of centuries.

Far different is it with those foreigners who settle in country districts where their children are under their constant oversight, and while the youngsters are learning the ways of America they are also held by their parents to industrious habits. Children of such immigrants become substantial citizens, while children of the same race brought up in the cities become a recruiting constituency for hoodlums, vagabonds, and criminals.

The reader must have observed in the preceding statistical estimates the startling preëminence of the negro in the ranks of criminals. His proportion of prisoners for adult males (13,219 per million) seems to be four times as great as that of the native stock, and more than twice as great as that of foreign parentage, while for boys his portion in the North Atlantic states (17,915 per million) is ten times as great as that of the corresponding native stock, and four times as great as that of foreign parentage.

The negro perhaps suffers by way of discrimination in the number of arrests and convictions compared with the whites, yet it is significant that in proportion to total numbers the negro prisoners in the Northern states are nearly twice as many as in the Southern states. Here, again, city life works its degenerating effects, for the Northern negroes are congregated mainly in towns and cities, while the Southern negroes remain in the country.

Did space permit, it would prove an interesting quest to follow the several races through the various classes of crime, noticing the relative seriousness of their offences, and paying attention to the female offenders. Only one class of offences can here be noted in detail; namely, that of public intoxication. Although classed as a crime, this offence borders on pauperism and the mental diseases, and its extreme prevalence indicates that the race in question is not overcoming the degenerating effects of competition and city life. Statistics from Massachusetts seem to show that drunkenness prevails to the greatest extent in the order of preëminence among the Irish, Welsh, English, and Scotch, and least among the Portuguese, Italians, Germans, Poles, and Jews. The Italians owe their prominence in the lists of prisoners to their crimes of violence, and very slightly to intoxication, though the latter is increasing among them. In the Southern states the ravages of drink among the negroes have been so severe and accompanied with such outbreaks of violence that the policy of prohibition of the liquor traffic has been carried farther than in any other section of the country. Probably three-fourths of the Southern negroes live in prohibition counties, and were it not for the paternal restrictions imposed by such laws, the downward course of the negro race would doubtless have outrun considerably the speed it has actually attained.

Besides the crimes which spring from racial tendencies, there is a peculiar class of crimes springing largely from race prejudice and hatred. These are lynchings and mob violence. The United States presents the paradox of a nation where respect for law and constitutional forms has won most signal triumphs, yet where concerted violations of law have been most widespread. By a queer inversion of thought, a crime committed jointly by many is not a crime, but a vindication of justice, just as a crime committed by authority of a nation is not a crime, but a virtue. Such crimes have not been continuous, but have arisen at times out of acute racial antagonisms. The Knownothing agitation of 1850 to 1855, which prevailed among religious and patriotic Americans, was directed against the newly arrived flood of immigrants from Europe and Asia, and was marked by a state of lawlessness and mob rule such as had never before existed, especially in the cities of Boston, New York, Pittsburg, Cincinnati, Louisville, and Baltimore. These subsided or changed their object under the oncoming slavery crisis, and the Civil War itself was a grand resort to violence by the South on a question of race domination. Beginning again with the Kuklux and White-cap uprisings in the seventies, mob rule drove the negroes back to a condition of subordination, but the lawless spirit then engendered has continued to show itself in the annual lynching of fifty to one hundred and fifty negroes suspected or convicted of the more heinous crimes. Nor has this crime of the mob been restricted to the South, but it has spread to the North, and has become almost the accepted code of procedure throughout the land wherever negroes are heinously accused. In the Northern instances this vengeance of the mob is sometimes wreaked on the entire race, for in the North the negro is more assertive, and defends his accused brother. But in the South the mob usually, though not always, stops with vengeance on the individual guilty, or supposedly guilty, since the race in general is already cowed.

Other races suffer at the hands of mobs, such as the Chinese in Wyoming and California at the hands of American mine workers, Italians in Louisiana and California at the hands of citizens and laborers, Slovaks and Poles in Latimer, Pennsylvania, at the hands of a mob militia. With the rise of organized labor these race riots and militia shootings increased in number, often growing out of the efforts of older races of workmen to drive newer and backward races from their jobs, or the efforts of employers to destroy newly formed unions of these immigrant races. Many strikes are accompanied by an incipient race war where employers are endeavoring to make substitution, one race for another, of Irish, Germans, native whites, Italians, negroes, Poles, and so on. Even the long series of crimes against the Indians, to which the term "A Century of Dishonor" seems to have attached itself without protest, must be looked upon as the mob spirit of a superior race bent on despoiling a despised and inferior race. That the frenzied spirit of the mob, whether in strikes, panicky militia, Indian slaughter, or civil war, should so often have blackened the face of a nation sincerely dedicated to law and order is one of the penalties paid for experimenting on a problem of political and economic equality with material marked by extreme racial inequality.

Poverty and Pauperism.—Prior to year 1875 the laws of the United States imposed no prohibition upon the immigration of paupers from foreign countries, and not until the federal government took from the states the administration of the law in 1891 did the prohibitions of the existing law become reasonably effective. Since that year there have been annually debarred, as likely to become public charges, 431 to 7898 arrivals, the latter number being debarred in the year 1905. In addition to those debarred at landing, there have been annually returned within one to three years after landing, 177 to 845 immigrants, many of whom had meantime become public charges. From these statements it will be seen that, prior to 1891, it was possible and quite probable that many thousand paupers and prospective paupers were admitted by the immigration authorities, and consequently the proportion of paupers among the foreign-born should appear larger than it would in later years. In the earlier years systematic arrangements were in force in foreign countries, especially Great Britain, to assist in the deportation of paupers to the United States, and therefore it is not surprising that, apart from race characteristics, there should have come to this country larger numbers of Irish paupers than those from any other nationality. Since these exportations have been stopped, it is not so much the actual pauper as the prospective pauper who gets admission. 96 per cent of the paupers in almshouses have been in this country ten years or more, showing that the exclusion laws are still defective, in that large numbers of poor physique are admitted. Taking the census reports for 1904, and confining our attention to the North Atlantic states, where children are generally provided for in separate establishments, we are able to compute the following as the relative extent of pauperism among males:—

Male Paupers in Almshouses Per Million Voting Population, North Atlantic States, 1904.

Native white, native parents	2,360
Native white, foreign parents	2,252
Foreign white	5,119
Colored	4,056

Here we see the counterpart of the estimates on crime, for the natives of foreign parentage show a smaller proportion of paupers than the natives of native parentage, while the foreign-born themselves show more than double the relative amount of pauperism of the native element, and the colored paupers are nearly twice the native stock.

The census bureau also furnishes computations showing the contributions of the different races and nationalities to the insane asylums and benevolent institutions. In general it appears that the foreign-born and the negroes exceed the native classes in their burden on the public. A report of the Department of Labor of great value and significance, incidentally bearing on this subject, shows for the Italians in Chicago their industrial and social conditions. According to this report the average earnings of Italians in that city in 1896 while at work were $6.41 per week for men and $2.11 per week for women, and the average time unemployed by the wage-earning element was over seven months. In another report of the Department of Labor it appears that the slum population of the cities of Baltimore, Chicago, New York, and Philadelphia in 1893 was unemployed three months each year. With wages one dollar a day, and employment only five months during the year, it is marvellous that the Italians of Chicago, during the late period of depression, were not thrown in great numbers upon public relief. Yet, with the strict administration of the exclusion laws leading to the deportation of over 2000 Italians a year as liable to become public charges, it is likely that the immigrants of that race, although low in physique, poverty, and standards of living, are fairly well screened of actual paupers.

CHAPTER VIII

POLITICS

American democracy was ushered in on a theory of equality. And no word has been more strangely used and abused. There is the monarchical idea of equality, and Mr. Mallock begs the question when he gives the title "Aristocracy and Evolution" to a book on the necessary part played by great men. Doubtless, in Greek, aristocracy means "government by the best," but in history it means government by the privilege of birth and landed property. Democracy may be in philology "government by the mob," but in politics and industry it has been opportunity for great men without blood or property. Mr. Münsterberg, too, sees the breakdown of American democracy and the reaction towards aristocracy in the prominence of civil-service reform, the preëminence conceded to business ability, the deference to wealth, and the conquest of the Philippines. But civil-service reform is only a device for opening the door to merit that has been shut by privilege. In England it was the means by which the mercantile classes broke into the offices preëmpted by the younger sons of aristocracy. In America it is an awkward means of admitting ability wherever found to positions seized upon by political usurpers. It appealed to the American democracy only when its advocates learned to call it, not "civil-service reform," but "the merit system." As for the astonishing power of mere wealth in American affairs the testimony of another English observer is based on wider observation when he says, "Even the tyranny of trusts is not to be compared with the tyranny of landlordism; for the one is felt to be merely an unhappy and (it is hoped) temporary aberration of well-meant social machinery, while the other seems bred in the very bone of the national existence."

A feeling of disappointment holds true of the conquest and treatment of the Philippines. That a war waged out of sympathy for an oppressed island nearby should have shaken down an unnoticed archipelago across the ocean was taken in childlike glee as the unexpected reward of virtue. But serious thinking has followed on seeing that these islands have added another race problem to the many that have thwarted democracy. Only a plutocracy sprung from race divisions at home could profit by race-subjection abroad, and the only alternative to race-subjection is equal representation in Congress. But to admit another race to partnership without the hope of assimilation is to reject experience. Independence or cession to Japan is the self-preservation of American democracy.

Another idea of equality is the socialist idea. Infatuated by an "economic interpretation of history," they overlook the racial interpretation. Permitting and encouraging plutocracy, they hope to see the dispossessed masses take possession when conditions become intolerable. But the "masses" would not be equal to the task. Privileged wealth knows too well how to buy up or promote their leaders, how to weaken them by internal dissensions, how to set race against race. Most of all, the inexperienced despotism of the masses is worse than the smooth despotism of wealth. The government of the South by the negro, the government of San Francisco by "labor," fell into the hands of the "carpet-bagger" and the "boss." Once in power, internal strife and jealousy, struggle for office, or racial antagonism disrupt the rulers, and a reaction throws them back more helpless than before. Men are not equal, neither are races or classes equal. True equality comes through equal opportunity. If individuals go forward, their race or class is elevated. They become spokesmen, defenders, examples. No race or class can rise without its own leaders. If they get admitted on equal terms with other leaders, whether it be in the councils of the church, the law-making bodies of the city, state, and nation, or the wage conferences of employers, they then can command the hearing which their abilities justify. They secure for their followers the equal opportunity to which they are entitled.

This is exactly the political problem that grows out of the presence of races and immigrants. With these admitted to the suffrage on the basis of mere manhood inspired by a generosity unknown to the people of any other land, the machinery of representative government inherited from England does not, for some reason, permit the free choice of leaders. The difficulties may be seen in cities where the system first broke down. A variety of races and nationalities living in the same ward are asked to elect aldermen and other officers by majority vote. No one nationality has a majority, but each sets up its list of candidates. The nationality with a mere plurality elects all of its candidates, and the other nationalities—a majority of the voters—are unrepresented. This is an extreme case, and has not often been allowed to happen. But the only means of preventing it is the "ward boss." The boss emerges from the situation as inevitably as the survival of the fittest. And the fittest is the Irishman. The Irishman has above all races the mixture of ingenuity, firmness, human sympathy, comradeship, and daring that makes him the amalgamator of races. He conciliates them all by nominating a ticket on which the offices are shrewdly distributed; and out of the Babel his "slate" gets the majority.

The boss's problem is not an easy one. His ward may contain business men on the hill and negroes along the canal. To nominate a business man would lose the negro vote—to nominate a negro would lose the business vote. He selects a nondescript somewhere between, and discards him for another at the next election. The representative becomes a tool in the hands of the boss. The boss sells his power to corporations, franchise speculators, and law-evaders. Representative democracy becomes bossocracy in the service of plutocracy. The ward system worked well when the suffrage was limited. Then the business men elected their business man unimpeded. But a system devised for restricted suffrage breaks down under universal suffrage. Could the ward lines be abolished, could the business men come together regardless of residence and elect their choice without the need of a majority vote, could the negroes and other races and classes do the same, then each would be truly represented by their natural leaders. So it is, not only in cities, but in county, state, and nation. Universal suffrage, clannish races, social classes, diversified interests, seem to explain and justify the presence of the party "machine" and its boss. Otherwise races, classes, and interests are in helpless conflict and anarchy. But the true explanation is an obsolete ward and district system of plurality representation adopted when but one race, class, or interest had the suffrage. Forms of government are the essence of government, notwithstanding the poet. An aristocratic form with a democratic suffrage is a plutocratic government. Belgium and Switzerland have shown that a democratic form is possible and practicable. Proportional representation instead of district representation is the corollary of universal suffrage which those countries have worked out as a model for others. The model is peculiarly adapted to a country of manifold nationalities, interests, and classes. Races and immigrants in America have not disproved democracy—they have proved the need of more democracy.

This is seen also in the distinction between men and measures. It often has been noted that in American elections the voters are more interested in voting for candidates than they are in voting on issues. The candidate arouses a personal and concrete interest—the issue is abstract and complicated. The candidate calls out a full vote—the issue is decided by a partial vote.

This difference is partly the result of organization. The candidate has a political party, campaign funds, and personal workers to bring out the vote. The issue has only its merits and demerits. Equally important under American conditions is the race or nationality of the candidate. This feature is often concealed by the ingenuity of political managers in nominating a ticket on which the several nationalities are "recognized." But with the recent progress of the movement to abolish party conventions and to nominate candidates directly at the primaries the racial prejudices of the voters show themselves. The nationalities line up for their own nationality, and the political and economic issues are thrown in the background. It is different when they vote on the issues directly. The vital questions of politics, industry, corporations, and monopoly which menace the country, unless rightly answered, cut across the lines of nationality. The German farmer, manufacturer, wage-earner, merchant, capitalist, and monopolist may all unite to elect a popular German to office, but they do not unite to give a corporation a monopoly. The same is true of other nationalities. Wherever the referendum has been fairly tested, in Chicago, Detroit, Oregon, and elsewhere, the sound judgment of all races has prevailed over bias, prejudice, or racial jealousy. There none can claim preëminence, for all have shown their share of patriotism, intelligence, and regard for equal rights. By an automatic self-disfranchisement the ignorant, the corrupt, and the indifferent of all races eliminate themselves by failing to vote. Instead of being dismissed on the ground that voters care mainly for men and less for measures, the referendum should be adopted on the ground that it permits those interested in measures to decide the question. Those who are not interested enough to vote do thereby proclaim that they are satisfied whichever side wins. The initiative and referendum are, above all other forms of government, the specific remedy for the ills of universal suffrage and conflicting nationalities. Race antagonism springs from personalities, race coalescence from community of interest. A vote for candidates intensifies antagonism—a vote on measures promotes community.

There are, indeed, some kinds of measures which stir up race antagonism. But the keenest of these have happily been eliminated. More intense than any other source of discord is religious belief. Religious differences in America are not so much theological as racial in character. The Judaism of the Jew, the Protestantism of the British and colonial American, the Lutheranism of the German, the Roman Catholicism of the Irish, Italian, and Slav, the Greek Catholicism of other Slavs, all testify to the history and psychology of races. Far-sighted indeed were our fathers who separated Church and State. Were the people taxed to support religion, every election would be a contest of races. All other questions would be subordinate, and democracy impossible. But with religion relegated to private judgment, each race is free to cultivate at will that one of its own peculiarities most fanatically adhered to, but most repellent to other races, while uniting with the others on what is most essential to democracy. Religious freedom is more than a private right—it is an American necessity.

Chinese Students, Honolulu
(From *The Independent*)

Another class of measures running partly along race lines are sumptuary laws, especially those regulating saloons and Sunday observance. In the Southern states saloon prohibition is largely a race discrimination and a race protection. In the North it often is American puritanism of the country against European liberalism of the cities. Here the referendum shows itself as the conciliator of nationalities. Upon no other issue has the popular vote been so generally resorted to. This issue comes close to the habits and passions of the masses. It takes precedence of all others except religion, but cannot be evaded like religion. If legislative bodies and executive officials decide the question, then the German or the Irishman adds to his zeal for the election of a conationalist his thirst for the election of a candidate with habits like his own. But when left to a popular vote, the saloon question is separated from the choice of candidates, and other issues come forward. A majority vote, too, pacifies the minority of all races, where the act of a legislative body leaves the suspicion of unfair advantage taken by unrepresentative politicians. By the exigencies of the situation the referendum has been invoked to take both the saloon problem and its share of the race problem "out of politics." The lesson is applicable wherever race or nationality conflicts with democracy. With questions of religious belief eliminated by the constitution, and questions of personal habits eliminated by the referendum, other questions of race antagonism will be eliminated by the initiative and the referendum.

Suffrage.—The climax of liberality in donating the suffrage to all races and conditions was reached with the fifteenth amendment in 1869. At that time not only had the negro been enfranchised; but nearly a score of Western and Southern states and territories had enfranchised the alien. So liberal were these states in welcoming the immigrant that they allowed him to vote as soon as he declared his intention to take out naturalization papers. This declaration, under the federal law, is made at least two years before the papers are granted, and it may be made as soon as the immigrant has landed. Thus in some of those states he could vote as soon as he acquired a legal residence, that is, four or four and one-half years before he acquired citizenship. Several of these states have recently changed these laws, but there remain nine that continue to accept the alien as a voter.

In the Eastern states such generosity was not granted by law but was practised by fraud. Naturalization papers are issued by federal courts and by state courts of record. The law gives the judge much discretion, for he is required to refuse the certificate if he is not satisfied that the alien is of good moral character, attached to the Constitution, and well disposed. But so careless or crowded are the judges that seldom have they examined the applicants. Indeed the political managers have had the option of judges and could take their immigrants to the court that would shut its eyes. Many thousands of fraudulent papers have been secured in this way, beginning at the very time when the naturalization law was enacted in 1802, but increasing enormously during the past forty years.

Finally, in 1906, Congress enacted a law giving to the Bureau of Immigration control over naturalization. The object is to bring all of the courts under a uniform practice, to provide complete records and means of identification, to establish publicity, to enable the government to appear in court and resist fraudulent naturalization, and to impose severe penalties. The law also adds something to the qualifications required of the alien. He must not be an anarchist or a polygamist, nor a believer of such doctrines; he must be able to speak the English language, and must intend to reside permanently in the United States. The language restriction affects but few, since in 1900 only 3.3 per cent of the naturalized foreign-born males of voting age could not speak English. The intention of permanent residence, as well as the entire measure, is designed to remove the abuse of foreigners' acquiring citizenship in order to return to their native land and defy their rightful government. On the administrative side this law is of great significance. It marks a serious beginning on the part of the federal government of protecting the citizenship that a generation before it had so liberally bestowed.

There are certain races which by law are prohibited from naturalization. For nearly seventy years the law on the subject enacted in 1802 admitted to citizenship only free white persons. This was amended in 1870 to admit "aliens of African nationality and persons of African descent." But other colored races were not admitted, so that the Chinese, Japanese, or Malay immigrant has never been eligible to citizenship. His children, however, born in this country are citizens, and cannot be excluded from voting on account of race or color. Indians living in tribes are foreigners, but if they recognize allegiance by paying taxes or dividing up their land in severalty they are citizens and voters.

Of the immigrant races eligible to citizenship their importance as possible voters is greater than their importance in the population. This is because men and boys come in greater numbers than women and children. Ten million foreign-born population furnishes 5,000,000 males of voting age, but 66,000,000 native population furnishes only 16,000,000 males of voting age. In other words, one-half of the foreign-born, and only one-fourth of the native-born, are potential voters. But not all of the potential voters are actual voters. With a grand total in the year 1900 of 21,000,000 of the proper sex and age, only 15,000,000 went to the polls. The ratio is five out of seven. Two million negroes were excluded, and 1,400,000 foreign-born had not yet naturalized. This leaves 2,600,000 natives and foreign-born who might have voted but did not. The foreigner who takes out his citizenship papers does it mainly to vote. Two-thirds of them had done so or declared their intention in 1900. Probably the proportion of native whites who did not vote was 15 per cent of their total number, and the proportion of foreign-born who did not, or could not, was over 40 per cent.

But this proportion differs greatly among the several races. It is not so much a difference in willingness as a difference in opportunity. Five years are required for naturalization, and while 40 per cent of those who have been here six to nine years have not declared their intention nor taken out their papers, only 7 per cent of those who have been here twenty years retain their allegiance to foreign governments. This increases relatively the political weight of the Teutonic and Celtic races which are oldest in point of immigration, and reduces relatively the weight of the Italian, Slav, and Jewish races. The figures below make this quite plain. The table shows the proportion of foreign-born who remain aliens, in the sense that they have neither taken out citizenship papers nor declared their intention of doing so. Only 7 to 13 per cent of the foreigners from Northwestern Europe are aliens, compared with 35 to 60 per cent of those from Eastern and Southern Europe. In course of time these differences will diminish, and the Italian and Slav will approach the Irishman and German in their share of American suffrage:—

Per cent of Aliens among Foreign-born Males of Voting Age

Wales	7.1
Germany	8.3
Norway	9.7
Ireland	10.1
Denmark	10.3
Holland	11.6
Sweden	11.9
Scotland	12.5
Bohemia	12.6
England	12.9
Canada, English	21.1
Russia (mainly Jews)	35.2
Canada, French	38.5
Finland	38.6
Austria (largely Slavs)	44.6
Portugal	51.6
Italy	53.0
Hungary (mainly Slavs)	53.1
Greece	57.8
Austria, Poland	61.

6

The right to vote is not "inalienable," neither is the right to life or liberty. Governments give them, refuse them, and take them away. In America this means the state governments. The federal government only declares that the states must follow the "due process of law," and not discriminate on account of race, religion, or servitude. In allowing the right to vote they may and do discriminate on other grounds, such as morals, illiteracy, intelligence, property, and sex. This may result in race or immigrant discrimination, and does so in the case of illiteracy and intelligence. After the Irish immigration of the forties, Connecticut in 1855 and Massachusetts in 1857 refused thenceforth to enfranchise those who could not read the Constitution. Since 1889 six other Northern and Western states—Wyoming, Maine, California, Washington, Delaware, and New Hampshire, in the order named—have erected barriers against those who cannot read or write the English language or the Constitution. Six Southern states have done the same, but one of them, Mississippi, has added another permanent barrier,—intelligence. This is supposed to be measured by ability to "understand" the Constitution as read by a white man. Southern states have also added vagrancy, poll tax, and property clauses even more exclusive than reading and writing. The federal courts have refused to interfere because these restrictions in their legal form bear alike on white and black. If in practice they bear unequally, that is a matter for the state courts.

To take away the suffrage from many of those who enjoy it is peacefully impossible under our system. But voters who hold fast to the privilege for themselves may be induced to deny it to the next generation. It was in this way usually that the foregoing restrictions were introduced. Massachusetts set the example by retaining all who could vote when the test was adopted, and making the exclusion apply only to those who came after. The Southern states did the same by "grandfather" and "understanding" clauses. By either method, in course of time, the favored voters disappear by death or removal, and the restrictions apply in full to the succeeding generation.

The effect of the educational test on the suffrage of the foreign-born is not as great as might be supposed. Naturalization itself is almost an educational test. Only 6.3 per cent of the naturalized foreigners are illiterate, but 28 per cent of those who remain aliens are unable to read. In Boston only 2 per cent are excluded from voting through inability to read English, although the corresponding aliens are 22 per cent. Probably the educational qualification in Massachusetts affects these proportions by lessening the inducement to naturalize, but in Chicago and New York, where that qualification is not required, scarcely more than 5 per cent of those who get naturalized would be unable to vote under such a law, compared with less than 1 per cent of the native voters. In the country at large the disproportion is not so great. Five and eight-tenths per cent of the sons of native parents would be excluded by an educational test against 6.3 per cent of the naturalized foreigners, and only 2 per cent of the native sons of foreigners. In the several Southern states the test, if equally applied, will exclude 6 to 20 per cent of the white voters and 35 to 60 per cent of the colored voters. In a Southern city like Memphis it would exclude 1 per cent of the white and 38 per cent of the colored.

Tested by the standards of democracy, the ability to read and write the English language is a proper qualification. It is perhaps the maximum that can be required, for to test the ability to understand what is read and written is to open the door to partisanship and race discrimination. Yet it is intelligence that makes the suffrage an instrument of protection, and it is not a denial of rights to refuse such an instrument to one who injures himself with it. The literacy qualification is one that can be acquired by effort. Other tests, especially the property qualification, are an assertion of inequality. Yet it is not strange that with the corrupt and inefficient governments that have accompanied universal suffrage there should have occurred a reaction. This has not always expressed itself in the policy of restricting the suffrage, for that can with difficulty be accomplished. It has shown itself rather in withdrawing government as far as possible from the control of the voters. The so-called "business theory" which has so generally been applied to the reform of city governments has converted the city as far as possible to the model of a private corporation, with its general manager, the mayor. The city has been denied its proper functions, and these have been turned over to private parties. But this reaction seems to have reached its limit. It is now understood to have been simply the legal recognition of an incipient plutocracy establishing itself under the forms of democracy. The return movement has begun, and the rescue of democracy is sought, as stated above, in forms and functions of government still more democratic.

The way plutocracy looks when it has passed the incipient stage may be seen in Hawaii. It is as though we had annexed those islands in order to watch in our own back yard the fruit of excessive immigration. A population of 154,000 furnishes 65,000 Hawaiians, Portuguese, and other Caucasians. The Chinese, Japanese, and Koreans have 87,000 population and no votes. The American contingent is some 17,000 souls and 3000 votes. The latter represent four classes or interests: the capitalist planters owning two-thirds of the property; superintendents, engineers, and foremen managing the plantation labor; skilled mechanics; small employers, merchants, and farmers. In order to get plantation labor and to keep the supply too large and diversified for concerted wage demands the planters imported contract Chinese in place of Hawaiians, then Japanese, then Koreans. As each race rises in standards and independence it leaves the plantations to enter trades, manufactures, and merchandising. It drives out the wage-earners from the less skilled occupations, then from the more skilled, then the small manufacturers, contractors, and merchants. The American middle classes disappear, partly by emigration to California, partly by abandoning business and relying on the values of real estate which rise through the competition of low standards of wages and profits, and partly by attaching themselves to the best-paid positions offered by the planters. In proportion as they move up in the scale through the entrance of immigrants in the lower positions, they transfer their allegiance from democracy to plutocracy. The planters themselves are caught in a circle. The rising values of their land absorb the high tariff on sugar and prevent rising wages if the values are to be kept up. The Japanese, with contract labor abolished, have shown a disposition to strike for higher wages. This has led to advances at the expense of profits, and the resulting "scarcity of labor" compels the planters again to ask for contract Chinese coolies. Immigration is thus only a makeshift remedy for the exactions of unions and the undevelopment of resources. More immigration requires perpetually more and still more, till the resulting plutocracy seeks to save itself by servile labor. A moderate amount of immigrant labor, assimilated and absorbed into the body politic, stimulates industry and progress, but an excessive and indigestible amount leads to the search for coercive remedies and ends in the stagnation of industry. The protective tariff was supposed to build up free American labor, but in Hawaii, with unrestricted immigration, it has handed us American plutocracy.

CHAPTER IX

AMALGAMATION AND ASSIMILATION

A German statistician, after studying population statistics of the United States and observing the "race suicide" of the native American stock, concludes: "The question of restriction on immigration is not a matter of higher or lower wages, nor a matter of more or less criminals and idiots, but the exclusion of a large part of the immigrants might cost the United States their place among the world powers."

Exactly the opposite opinion was expressed in 1891 by Francis A. Walker, the leading American statistician of his time, and superintendent of the censuses of 1870 and 1880. He said: "Foreign immigration into this country has, from the time it first assumed large proportions, amounted not to a reinforcement of our population, but a replacement of native by foreign stock.... The American shrank from the industrial competition thus thrust upon him. He was unwilling himself to engage in the lowest kind of day labor with these new elements of population; he was even more unwilling to bring sons and daughters into the world to enter into that competition.... The more rapidly foreigners came into the United States, the smaller was the rate of increase, not merely among the native population separately, but throughout the population of the country as a whole," including the descendants of the earlier foreign immigrants.

Walker's statements of fact, whatever we may say of his explanations, are easily substantiated. From earliest colonial times until the census of 1840 the people of the United States multiplied more rapidly than the people of any other modern nation, not excepting the prolific French Canadians. The first six censuses, beginning in 1790, show that, without appreciable immigration, the population doubled every twenty years, and had this rate of increase continued until the present time, the descendants of the colonial white and negro stock in the year 1900 would have numbered 100,000,000 instead of the combined colonial, immigrant, and negro total of 76,000,000. Indeed, if we take the total immigration from 1820 to 1900, exceeding 19,000,000 people, and apply a slightly higher than the average rate of increase from births, we shall find that in the year 1900 one-half of the white population is derived from immigrant stock, leaving the other half, or but 33,000,000 whites, derived from the colonial stock. This is scarcely more than one-third of the number that should have been expected had the colonial element continued to multiply from 1840 to 1900 as it had multiplied from 1790 to 1840.

An interesting corroboration of these speculations is the prediction made in the year 1815, thirty years before the great migration of the nineteenth century, by the mathematician and publicist, Elkanah Watson. On the basis of the increase shown in the first three censuses he made computations of the probable population for each census year to 1900, and I have drawn up the following table, showing the actual population compared with his estimates. Superintendent Walker, in the essay above quoted, uses Watson's figures, and points out the remarkable fact that those predictions were within less than one per cent of the actual population until the year 1860, although, meanwhile, there had come nearly 5,000,000 immigrants whom Watson could not have foreseen. Thus the population of 1860, notwithstanding access of the millions of immigrants, was only 310,000, or one per cent less than Watson had predicted. And the falling off since 1860 has been even greater, for, notwithstanding the immigration of 20,000,000 persons since 1820, the population in 1900 was 75,000,000, or 25 per cent less than Watson's computations.

POPULATION AND IMMIGRATION

Population (Census)	Watson's Estimate	Watson's Error	Foreign Immigration for Decade

1790	3,929,214			
1800	5,308,483			50,000
1810	7,239,881			70,000
1820	9,633,822	9,625,734	-8,088	114,000
1830	12,866,020	12,833,645	-32,375	143,439
1840	17,069,453	17,116,526	+47,073	599,125
1850	23,191,876	23,185,368	-6,508	1,713,251
1860	31,443,321	31,753,825	+310,503	2,598,214
1870	38,558,371	42,328,432	+3,770,061	2,314,824
1880	50,155,783	56,450,241	+6,294,458	2,812,191
1890	62,622,250	77,266,989	+14,644,739	5,246,613
1900	75,559,258	100,235,985	+24,676,727	3,687,564
Total immigration 1820-1900				19,229,224

This question of the "race suicide" of the American or colonial stock should be regarded as the most fundamental of our social problems, or rather as the most fundamental consequence of our social and industrial institutions. It may be met by exhortation, as when President Roosevelt says, "If the men of the nation are not anxious to work in many different ways, with all their might and strength, and ready and able to fight at need, and anxious to be fathers of families, and if the women do not recognize that the greatest thing for any woman is to be a good wife and mother, why that nation has cause to be alarmed about its future."

The anxiety of President Roosevelt is well grounded; but if race suicide is not in itself an original cause, but is the result of other causes, then exhortation will accomplish but little, while the removal or amelioration of the other causes will of itself correct the resulting evil. Where, then, shall we look for the causes of race suicide, or, more accurately speaking, for the reduced proportion of children brought into the world? The immediate circumstances consist in postponing the age of marriage, in limiting the number of births after marriage, and in an increase in the proportion of unmarried people. The reasons are almost solely moral and not physical. Those who are ambitious and studious, who strive to reach a better position in the world for themselves and their children, and who have not inherited wealth, will generally postpone marriage until they have educated themselves, or accumulated property, or secured a permanent position. They will then not bring into the world a larger number of children than they can provide for on the basis of the standing which they themselves have attained; for observation shows that those who marry early have large families, and are generally kept on a lower station in life. The real problem, therefore, with this class of people, is the opportunities for earning a living. In the earlier days, when the young couple could take up vacant land, and farming was the goal of all, a large family and the coöperation of wife and children were a help rather than a hindrance. To-day the couple, unless the husband has a superior position, must go together to the factory or mill, and the children are a burden until they reach the wage-earning age. Furthermore, wage-earning is uncertain, factories shut down, and the man with a large family is thrown upon his friends or charity. To admonish people living under these conditions to go forth and multiply is to advise the cure of race suicide by race deterioration.

Faculty of Tuskegee Institute
(From *World's Work*)

Curiously enough, these observations apply with even greater force to the second generation of immigrants than to the native stock, for among the daughters of the foreign-born only 19 per cent of those aged 15 to 24 years are married, while among daughters of native parents 30 per cent are married; and for the men of 20 to 29 only 26.8 per cent of the native sons of foreigners are married and 38.5 per cent of the sons of natives. These figures sustain what can be observed in many large cities, that the races of immigrants who came to this country twenty-five or more years ago are shrinking from competition with the new races from Southern Europe.

Boston, for example, with its large Irish immigration beginning two generations ago, shows a similar disproportion. Of the American daughters of foreign parents 15 to 24 years of age, only 12 per cent are married, but of the daughters of native parents 17 per cent are married; of the sons of foreign parents 20 to 29 years of age, only 20 per cent are married, but of the sons of native parents 26 per cent are married. The contrast with the immigrants themselves is striking. In Boston, 24 per cent of the foreign-born women aged 15 to 24 are married, and 35 per cent of the foreign-born men aged 20 to 29. In other words, the early marriages of immigrant men and women are nearly twice as many as those of the American-born sons and daughters of immigrants, and only one-third more than those of the sons and daughters of native stock. With such a showing as this it would seem that our "place among the world powers" depends indeed on immigration, for the immigrants' children are more constrained to race suicide than the older American stock.

The competition is not so severe in country districts where the native stock prevails; but in the cities and industrial centres the skilled and ambitious workman and workwoman discover that in order to keep themselves above the low standards of the immigrants they must postpone marriage. The effect is noticeable and disastrous in the case of the Irish-Americans. Displaced by Italians and Slavs, many of the young men have fallen into the hoodlum and criminal element. Here moral causes produce physical causes of race destruction, for the vicious elements of the population disappear through the diseases bequeathed to their progeny, and are recruited only from the classes forced down from above. On the other hand, many more Irish have risen to positions of foremanship, or have lived on their wits in politics, or have entered the priesthood. The Irish-American girls, showing independence and ambition, have refused to marry until they could be assured of a husband of steady habits, and they have entered clerical positions, factories, and mills. Thus this versatile race, with distinct native ability, is meeting in our cities the same displacement and is resorting to the same race suicide which itself inflicted a generation or two earlier on the native colonial stock. But the effect is more severe, for the native stock was able to leave the scenes of competition, to go West and take up farms or build cities, but the Irish-American has less opportunity to make such an escape.

Great numbers of Irishmen, together with others of English, Scotch, German, and American descent, remaining in these industrial centres, have sought to protect themselves and maintain high standards through labor-unions and the so-called "closed shop," by limiting the number of apprentices, excluding immigrants, and giving their sons a preference of admission. But even with the unions they find it necessary also to limit the size of their families, and I am convinced from personal observation, that, were the statistics on this point compiled from the unions of skilled workmen, there would be found even stronger evidences of race suicide than among other classes in the nation.

To the well-to-do classes freedom from the care of children is not a necessity, but an opportunity for luxury and indulgence. These include the very wealthy, whose round of social functions would be interrupted by home obligations. To them, of course, immigration brings no need of prudence—it rather helps to bring the enormous fortunes which distract their attention from the home. But their numbers are insignificant compared with the millions who determine the fate of the nation. More significant are the well-to-do farmers and their wives who have inherited the soil redeemed by their fathers, and whose desire to be free for enjoying the fruits of civilization lead them to the position so strongly condemned by President Roosevelt. This class of farmers, as shown in the census map of the size of private families, may be traced across the Eastern and Northern states, running through New England, rural New York, Northern Pennsylvania, Ohio, and Michigan, parts of Indiana, Illinois, Wisconsin, and Iowa. In the rich counties of southern Michigan, settled and occupied mainly by native stock from New York, the average size of families is less than four persons, as it is in a large area of Central New York, whereas for the country at large it is 4.7, and for counties in the mining sections of Michigan occupied by immigrants it rises as high as 5.8 persons.

The census figures showing the size of families do not, however, reveal the number of children born to a family, since they show only those living together and not those who have moved away or died. This especially affects the large-sized families, and does not reveal, for example, a fact shown by Kuczynski from the state census of Massachusetts that the average number of children of the foreign-born women in that state is 4.5, while for native women it is only 2.7. This also affects the showing for a state like West Virginia, composed almost entirely of native Americans of colonial stock, with only 2 per cent foreign-born and 5 per cent colored, where the average size of families is 5.1

persons, the highest in the United States, but where in the Blue Ridge Mountains I have come upon two couples of native white Americans who claimed respectively eighteen and twenty-two children. Throughout the South the reduction in size of families and the postponement of marriage have not occurred to any great extent either among the white or colored races, and these are states to which immigration has contributed less than 3 per cent of their population. Yet, if Superintendent Walker's view is sound in all respects, the Southern whites should shrink from competition with the negro in the same way that the Northern white shrinks from competition with the immigrant. He does not do so, and the reasons are probably found in the fact that the South has been remote from the struggle of modern competition, and that ignorance and proud contentment fail to spur the masses to that ambitious striving which rises by means of what Malthus called the prudential restraints on population. It is quite probable that in the South, with the spread of the factory system and universal education, the growth in numbers through excess of births over deaths will be retarded.

On the whole it seems that immigration and the competition of inferior races tends to dry up the older and superior races wherever the latter have learned to aspire to an improved standard of living, and that among well-to-do classes not competing with immigrants, but made wealthier by their low wages, a similar effect is caused by the desire for luxury and easy living.

Americanization.—A line on the chart opposite page 63 shows the proportions between the number of immigrants and the existing population. From this it appears that the enormous immigration of 1906 is relatively not as large as the smaller immigration of the years 1849 to 1854, or the year 1882. Three hundred thousand immigrants in 1850 was as large an addition to a population of 23,000,000 as 1,000,000 in 1906 to a population of 85,000,000. Judged by mere numbers, the present immigration is not greater than that witnessed by two former periods. Judged by saturation it may be greater, for the former immigrants were absorbed by colonial Americans, but the present immigrants enter a solution half colonial and half immigrant. The problem of Americanization increases more than the number to be Americanized. What is the nature of this problem, and what are the forces available for its solution?

The term amalgamation may be used for that mixture of blood which unites races in a common stock, while assimilation is that union of their minds and wills which enables them to think and act together. Amalgamation is a process of centuries, but assimilation is a process of individual training. Amalgamation is a blending of races, assimilation a blending of civilizations. Amalgamation is beyond the organized efforts of government, but assimilation can be promoted by social institutions and laws. Amalgamation therefore cannot attract our practical interest, except as its presence or absence sets limits to our efforts toward assimilation.

Our principal interest in amalgamation is its effect on the negro race. The census statisticians discontinued after 1890 the inquiry into the number of mulattoes, but the census of 1890 showed that mulattoes were 15 per cent of the total negro population. This was a slightly larger proportion than that of preceding years. The mulatto element of the negro race is almost a race of itself. Its members on the average differ but little if at all from those of the white race in their capacity for advancement, and it is the tragedy of race antagonism that they with their longings should suffer the fate of the more contented and thoughtless blacks. In their veins runs the blood of white aristocracy, and it is a curious psychology of the Anglo-Saxon that assigns to the inferior race those equally entitled to a place among the superior. But sociology offers compensation for the injustice to physiology. The mulatto is the natural leader, instructor, and spokesman of the black. Prevented from withdrawing himself above the fortunes of his fellows, he devotes himself to their elevation. This fact becomes clear in proportion as the need of practical education becomes clear. The effective work of the whites through missionary schools and colleges has not been the elevation of the black, but the elevation of mulattoes to teach the blacks. A new era for the blacks is beginning when the mulatto sees his own future in theirs.

Apart from the negro we have very little knowledge of the amalgamation of races in America. We only know that for the most part they have blended into a united people with harmonious ideals, and the English, the German, the Scotch-Irish, the Dutch, and the Huguenot have become the American.

We speak of superior and inferior races, and this is well enough, but care should be taken to distinguish between inferiority and backwardness—between that superiority which is the original endowment of race and that which results from the education and training which we call civilization. While there are superior and inferior races, there are primitive, mediæval, and modern civilizations, and there are certain mental qualities required for and produced by these different grades of civilization. A superior race may have a primitive or mediæval civilization, and therefore its individuals may never have exhibited the superior mental qualities with which they are actually endowed, and which a modern civilization would have called into action. The adults coming from such a civilization seem to be inferior in their mental qualities, but their children, placed in the new environments of the advanced civilization, exhibit at once the qualities of the latter. The Chinaman comes from a mediæval civilization—he shows little of those qualities which are the product of Western civilization, and with his imitativeness, routine, and traditions, he has earned the reputation of being entirely non-assimilable. But the children of Chinamen, born and reared in this country, entirely disprove this charge, for they are as apt in absorbing the spirit and method of American institutions as any Caucasian. The race is superior but backward.

The Teutonic races until five hundred years after Christ were primitive in their civilization, yet they had the mental capacities which made them, like Arminius, able to comprehend and absorb the highest Roman civilization. They passed through the mediæval period and then came out into the modern period of advanced civilization, yet during these two thousand years their mental capacities, the original endowment of race, have scarcely improved. It is civilization, not race evolution, that has transformed the primitive warrior into the philosopher, scientist, artisan, and business man. Could their babies have been taken from the woods two thousand years ago and transported to the homes and schools of modern America, they could have covered in one generation the progress of twenty centuries. Other races, like the Scotch and the Irish, made the transition from primitive institutions to modern industrial habits within a single century, and Professor Brinton, our most profound student of the American Indian, has said, "I have been in close relations to several full-blood American Indians who had been removed from an aboriginal environment and instructed in this manner, and I could not perceive that they were either in intellect or sympathies inferior to the usual type of the American gentleman. One of them notably had a refined sense of humor as well as uncommon acuteness of observation."

The line between superior and inferior, as distinguished from advanced and backward, races appears to be the line between the temperate and tropical zones. The two belts of earth between the tropics of Capricorn and Cancer and the arctic and antarctic circles have been the areas where man in his struggle for existence developed the qualities of mind and will—the ingenuity, self-reliance, self-control, strenuous exertion, and will power—which befit the modern industrial civilization. But in the tropics these qualities are less essential, for where nature lavishes food, and winks at the neglect of clothing and shelter, there ignorance, superstition, physical prowess, and sexual passion have an equal chance with intelligence, foresight, thrift, and self-control. The children of all the races of the temperate zones are eligible to the highest American civilization, and it only needs that they be "caught" young enough. There is perhaps no class of people more backward than the 3,000,000 poor whites of the Appalachian Mountains, but there is no class whose children are better equipped by heredity to attain distinction in any field of American endeavor. This much cannot be said for the children of the tropical zones. Amalgamation is their door to assimilation.

Before we can intelligently inquire into the agencies of Americanization we must first agree on what we mean by the term. I can think of no comprehensive and concise description equal to that of Abraham Lincoln: "Government of the people, by the people, for the people." This description should be applied not only to the state but to other institutions. In the home it means equality of husband and wife; in the church it means the voice of the laity; in industry the participation of the workmen.

Unhappily it cannot be said that Lincoln's description has ever been attained. It is the goal which he and others whom we recognize as true Americans have pointed out. Greater than any other obstacle in the road toward that goal have been our race divisions. Government for the people depends on government by the people, and this is difficult where the people cannot think and act together. Such is the problem of Americanization.

In the earlier days the most powerful agency of assimilation was frontier life. The pioneers "were left almost entirely to their own resources in this great struggle. They developed a spirit of self-reliance, a capacity for self-government, which are the most prominent characteristics of the American people." Frontier life includes pioneer mining camps as well as pioneer farming.

Next to the frontier the farms of America are the richest field of assimilation. Here the process is sometimes thought to be slower than it is in the cities, but any one who has seen it under both conditions cannot doubt that if it is slower it is more real. In the cities the children are more regularly brought under the influence of the public schools, but more profound and lasting than the education of the schools is the education of the street and the community. The work of the schools in a great city like New York cannot be too highly praised, and without such work the future of the immigrant's child would be dark. In fact the children of the immigrant are better provided with school facilities than the children of the Americans. Less than 1 per cent of their children 10 to 14 years of age are illiterate, but the proportion of illiterates among children of native parents is over 4 per cent. This is not because the foreigner is more eager to educate his child than is the native, but because nearly three-fourths of the foreigners' children and only one-sixth of the natives' children live in the larger cities, where schools and compulsory attendance prevail. Were it not for compulsory education, the child of the peasant immigrant would be, like the child of the Slav in the anthracite coal fields, "the helpless victim of the ignorance, frugality, and industrial instincts of his parents." As it is, they drop out of the schools at the earliest age allowed by law, and the hostility of foreigners to factory legislation and its corollary compulsory school legislation is more difficult to overcome than the hostility of American employers, both of whom might profit by the work of their children. The thoroughness with which the great cities of the North enforce the requirements of primary education leaves but little distinction between the children of natives and the children of foreigners, but what difference remains is to the advantage of the natives. In Boston in 1900 only 5 children of native parents were illiterate, and 22 native children of foreign parents, a ratio of one-twentieth of 1 per cent for the natives and one-tenth of 1 per cent for the foreigners. In New York 68 of the 83,000 children of native parents were illiterate, and 311 of the 166,000 native children of foreign parents, a ratio insignificant in both cases, but more than twice as great for the foreigners as for the natives. Taking all of the cities of at least 50,000 population, more than one-fourth of the foreign-born children 10 to 15 years of age are bread-winners, and only one-tenth of the children of native parents. The influence of residence in America is shown by the fact that of the children of foreigners born in this country the proportion of bread-winners is reduced to one-seventh.

But it is the community more than the school that gives the child his actual working ideals and his habits and methods of life. And in a great city, with its separation of classes, this community is the slums, with its mingling of all races and the worst of the Americans. He sees and knows surprisingly little of the America that his school-books describe. The American churches, his American employers, are in other parts of the city, and his Americanization is left to the school-teacher, the policeman, and the politician, who generally are but one generation before him from Europe. But on the farm he sees and knows all classes, the best and the worst, and even where his parents strive to isolate their community and to preserve the language and the methods of the old country, only a generation or two are required for the surrounding Americanism to permeate. Meanwhile healthful work, steady, industrious, and thrifty habits, have made him capable of rising to the best that his surroundings exemplify.

Slavic Home Missionaries
(From *The Home Missionary*)

Since the year 1900 the Immigration Bureau has not inquired as to the religious faith of the immigrants. In that year, when the number admitted was 361,000, one-fifth were Protestants, mainly from Great Britain, the Scandinavian countries, Germany, and Finland. One-tenth were Jews, 4 per cent were Greek Catholics, and 52 per cent were Roman Catholics. With the shifting of the sources toward the east and south of Europe the proportion of Catholic and Jewish faith has increased. During this transition the Protestant churches of America have begun to awaken to a serious problem confronting them. The three New England states which have given their religion and political character to Northern and Western states are themselves now predominantly Catholic. In all of the Northern manufacturing and industrial states and in their great cities the marvellous organization and discipline of the Roman Catholic Church has carefully provided every precinct, ward, or district with chapels, cathedrals, and priests even in advance of the inflow of population, while the scattered forces of Protestantism overlap in some places and overlook other places. Two consequences have followed. The Protestant churches in much the larger part of their activities have drawn themselves apart in an intellectual and social round of polite entertainment for the families of the mercantile, clerical, professional, and employing classes, while the Catholic churches minister to the laboring and wage-earning classes. In a minor and relatively insignificant part of their activities the Protestant churches have supported missionaries, colporters, and chapels among the immigrants, the wage-earners, and their children. Their home missionary societies, which in the earlier days followed up their own believers on the frontier and enabled them to establish churches in their new homes, have in the past decade or two become foreign missionary societies working at home. Nothing is more significant or important in the history of American Protestantism than the zeal and patriotism with which a few missionaries in this unaccustomed field have begun to lead the way. By means of addresses, periodicals, books, study classes, they are gradually awakening the churches to the needs of the foreigner at home. Among certain nationalities, especially the Italians and Slavs, they find an open field, for thousands of those nationalities, though nominally Catholic, are indifferent to the church that they associate with oppression at home. Among these nationalities already several converts have become missionaries in turn to their own people, and with the barrier of language and suspicion thus bridged over, the influence of the Protestant religion is increasing. Perhaps more than anything else is needed a federation of the Protestant denominations similar to that recently arranged in Porto Rico. That island has been laid out in districts through mutual agreement of the home missionary societies, and each district is assigned exclusively to a single denomination.

While the Protestant churches have been withdrawing from the districts invaded by the foreigners, the field has been entered by the "social settlement." This remarkable movement, eliminating religious propaganda, is essentially religious in its zeal for social betterment. Its principal service has been to raise up Americans who know and understand the life and needs of the immigrants and can interpret them to others. In the "institutional church" is also to be found a similar adaptation of the more strictly religious organization to the social and educational needs of the immigrants and their children.

More than any other class in the community, it is the employers who determine the progress of the foreigner and his children towards Americanization. They control his waking hours, his conditions of living, and his chances of advancement. In recent years a few employers have begun to realize their responsibilities, and a great corporation like the Colorado Fuel and Iron Company establishes its "sociological" department with its schools, kindergartens, hospitals, recreation centres, and model housing, on an equal footing with its engineering and sales departments. Other employers are interesting themselves in various degrees and ways in "welfare work," or "industrial betterment," and those who profit most by this awakening interest are the foreign-born and their families. This interest has not yet shown itself in a willingness to shorten the hours of labor, and this phase of welfare work must probably be brought about by other agencies.

The influence of schools, churches, settlements, and farming communities applies more to the children of immigrants than their parents. The immigrants themselves are too old for Americanization, especially when they speak a non-English language. To them the labor-union is at present the strongest Americanizing force. The effort of organized labor to organize the unskilled and the immigrant is the largest and most significant fact of the labor movement. Apart from the labor question itself, it means the enlistment of a powerful self-interest in the Americanization of the foreign-born. For it is not too much to say that the only effective Americanizing force for the Southeastern European is the labor-union. The church to which he gives allegiance is the Roman Catholic, and, however much the Catholic Church may do for the ignorant peasant in his European home, such instruction as the priest gives is likely to tend toward an acceptance of their subservient position on the part of the workingmen. It is a frequently observed fact that when immigrants join a labor-union they almost insolently warn the priest to keep his advice to himself.

Universal suffrage admits the immigrant to American politics within one to five years after landing. But the suffrage is not looked upon to-day as the sufficient Americanizing force that a preceding generation imagined. The suffrage appeals very differently to the immigrant voter and to the voter who has come up through the American schools and American life. The American has learned not only that this is a free government, but that its freedom is based on constitutional principles of an abstract nature. Freedom of the press, trial by jury, separation of powers, independence of the judiciary, equality of opportunity, and several other governmental and legal principles have percolated through his subconscious self, and when he contemplates public questions these abstract principles have more or less influence as a guide to his ballot. But the immigrant has none of these. He comes here solely to earn a better living. The suffrage is nothing to him but a means of livelihood. Not that he readily sells his vote for money—rather does he simply "vote for his job." He votes as instructed by his employer or his political "boss," because it will help his employer's business or because his boss will get him a job, or will, in some way, favor him and others of his nationality. There is a noticeable difference between the immigrant and the children of the immigrant in this regard. The young men, when they begin to vote, can be appealed to on the ground of public spirit; their fathers can be reached only on the ground of private interest.

Now it cannot be expected that the labor-union or any other influence will greatly change the immigrant in this respect. But the union does this much: it requires every member to be a citizen, or to have declared his intention of taking out naturalization papers. The reasons for doing this are not political; they are sentimental and patriotic. The union usually takes pride in showing that its members are Americans, and have foregone allegiance to other countries. In a union like the musicians' the reasons for requiring citizenship are also protective, since they serve to exclude transient musical immigrants from American audiences. Again, the union frees its members from the dictation of employers, bosses, and priests. Politicians, of course, strive to control the vote of organized labor, but so disappointing has been the experience of the unions that they have quite generally come to distrust the leader who combines labor and politics. The immigrant who votes as a unionist has taken the first step, in casting his ballot, towards considering the interests of others, and this is also the first step towards giving public spirit and abstract principles a place alongside private interest and his own job.

But there is another way, even more impressive, in which the union asserts the preëminence of principles over immediate self-interest. When the foreigner from Southern Europe is inducted into the union, then for the first time does he get the idea that his job belongs to him by virtue of a right to work, and not as the personal favor or whim of a boss. These people are utterly obsequious before their foremen or bosses, and it is notorious that nearly always they pay for the privilege of getting and keeping a job. This bribery of bosses, as well as the padrone system, proceed from the deep-seated conviction that despotism is the natural social relation, and that therefore they must make terms with the influential superior who is so fortunate as to have favor with the powers that be.

The anthracite coal operators represented such men, prior to joining the union, as disciplined and docile workmen, but in doing so they disregarded the fact that outside the field where they were obsequious they were most violent, treacherous, and factional. Before the organization of the union in the coal fields these foreigners were given over to the most bitter and often murderous feuds among the ten or fifteen nationalities and the two or three factions within each nationality. The Polish worshippers of a given saint would organize a night attack on the Polish worshippers of another saint; the Italians from one province would have a knife for the Italians of another province, and so on. When the union was organized the antagonisms of race, religion, and faction were eliminated. The immigrants came down to an economic basis and turned their forces against their bosses. "We fellows killed this country," said a Polish striker to Father Curran, "and now we are going to make it." The sense of a common cause, and, more than all else, the sense of individual rights as men, have come to these people through the organization of their labor unions, and it could come in no other way, for the union appeals to their necessities, while other forces appeal to their prejudices. They are even yet far from ideal Americans, but those who have hitherto imported them and profited by their immigration should be the last to cry out against the chief influence that has started them on the way to true Americanism.

Agricultural Distribution of Immigrants.—The congestion and colonizing of immigrants in the cities and their consequent poverty and the deterioration of the second generation have brought forth various proposals for inducing them to settle upon the farms. The commissioners of immigration at various times have advocated an industrial museum at Ellis Island, wherein the resources and opportunities of the several states could be displayed before the eyes of the incoming thousands. They and others have gone further and advocated the creation of a bureau of immigrant distribution to help the immigrants out of the crowded cities into the country districts. Still others have urged the establishment of steamship lines to Southern ports and the Gulf of Mexico, so that immigrants may be carried directly to the regions that "need them." Very little can be expected from projects of this kind, for the present contingent of immigrants from Southeastern Europe is too poor in worldly goods and too ignorant of American business to warrant an experiment in the isolation and self-dependence of farming. The farmers of the South and West welcome the settler who has means of purchase, but they distrust the newly arrived immigrant. Scandinavians and Germans in large numbers find their way to their countrymen on the farms, but the newer nationalities would require the fostering care of government or of wealthy private societies. The Jews have, indeed, taken up the matter, and the Jewish Agricultural and Industrial Aid Society of New York, by means of subventions from the Baron de Hirsch fund, has distributed many families throughout the country, partly in agriculture, but more generally in trade. The Society for the Protection of Italian Immigrants is doing similar work. Great railway systems and land companies in the South and West have their agricultural and industrial agents on the lookout for eligible settlers. All of the Southern states have established bureaus of immigration, and they are advertising the North and Europe for desirable immigrants. But these agencies seek mainly those immigrants who have resided in the country for a time, and have learned the language and American practices, and, in the case of the railroad and land companies, those who have accumulated some property.

The immigration bureaus of the Southern states and railways, the most urgent applicants at the present time for immigrants, are strongly opposed to the plan of federal distribution. They want farmers who will do their own work. From the standpoint of the immigrant himself this position is correct. To find a place as an agriculturist he must find a place as a farmer and not a harvest hand. Speaking for the Southern bureaus, Professor Fleming says, "The South decidedly objects to being made the government dumping-ground for undesirable immigrants. It does not want the lower class foreigners who have swarmed into the Northern cities. It wants the same sort of people who settled so much of the West." The state board of South Carolina officially invites immigration of "white citizens of the United States, citizens of Ireland, Scotland, Switzerland, and France, and all other foreigners of Saxon origin."

As for those without money who must depend on their daily labor for wages, they must go where employment is most regular and the best wages are paid. This is not on the farms, with a few months' work in summer and no homes in winter. It is unmistakably in the great cities and industrial centres. The commissioner of immigration at Ellis Island, speaking of the cordon established by his bureau along the Canadian frontier from Halifax to Winnipeg in order to catch those who tried to escape inspection at New York, said, "All those immigrants who had New York, Philadelphia, Chicago, Cleveland, or Cincinnati in mind as a destination when they left Europe and came to Quebec, went all the way around that wall to its western end at Winnipeg, and then took trains and came back to the very places they had in mind when they left Europe; and if you were to land all the ships that now come to New York at Galveston, New Orleans, or Charleston, every one of the immigrants would come to the place he had in mind when he decided to emigrate."

Professor Wilcox contends that the immigrants already distribute themselves according to their economic advantage as completely as do the natives. They seem to congest in the cities because the cities are necessarily their places of first arrival. "Our foreign-born arrive, in at least nine-tenths of the cases, at some city. Our native citizens arrive by birth, in at least three-fourths of the cases, in the country. The foreign-born arrive mainly at seaport cities, and disperse gradually from those cities to and through other interior cities, ultimately reaching in many cases the small towns or open country. It is in no sense surprising, or an evidence of imperfect distribution, that the foreign-born should be massed in the cities when nine-tenths of them arrive there, and the native population massed in the country districts when three-fourths of them arrive there." Artificial distribution would not relieve the pressure as long as the character and amount of immigration continue—it can only be relieved by creating greater economic inducements in the country. Natives and foreigners both crowd to the cities because wages and profits are higher than they are in the country.

Even supposing the congestion in the cities could be relieved by making the inducements in the country greater, the relief could not continue, for it would only invite more immigration. Emigration has not relieved the pressure of population in Europe. In no period of their history, with the exception of Ireland, have the populations of Europe increased at a greater rate than during the last half century of migration to America. It is not emigration but improved standards of living that lessens the pressure of numbers, and France with the widest diffusion of property has little emigration and no increase in population. With the redundant millions of Europe, increasing thousands would migrate if they got word from their friends that the American government is finding jobs for them. Just as we have already seen that the tide of immigration rises with a period of prosperity in America, so would it rise with agricultural distribution of immigrants. Both are simply more openings for employment, and the knowledge of such opportunities is promptly carried to the waiting multitudes abroad.

Consider also the political jeopardy of an administration at Washington conducting a bureau for the distribution of immigrants. If it refused to direct immigrants to one section of the country because it found that the wages were low, it would arouse the hostility of employers. If it directed them to another section, where the wages offered were high because the employers were preparing for a lockout, or the unions were on strike, it would lose the votes of workingmen. The administration would soon learn that safely to conduct such a bureau it must not conduct it at all.

Far better is it that the federal government should leave the distribution of immigrants to private employment agencies. It might then license all such agencies that conduct an interstate business. With the power to take away the license on proof of fraud and misrepresentation, and with the prosecution of agencies and employers that deceive and enslave the immigrant, the government would accomplish all that it could directly do for better distribution. Unquestionably the employment agencies, with their *padroni*, their bankers, and their false promises, are the source of miserable abuse to thousands of immigrants. They require interstate as well as state regulation. By weeding out the dishonest agencies the field would be occupied by the honest ones, and the immigrant could trust himself to their assistance. But such regulation would not be merely for the sake of the immigrant. It would, as it should, aid the American as well.

This suggests to us the true nature of the problem of city congestion and the nature of its solution. It is not to be found in special efforts on behalf of the immigrant, but in efforts to better the condition of both Americans and immigrants. The congestion of cities is owing to discriminations in favor of cities. If the government gives aid to agriculture as it does to manufactures, if it provides better communication, equalizes taxes, reduces freight rates to the level enjoyed by cities, then agriculture and the small towns will be more attractive. Americans will not crowd to the cities, and the more provident of the immigrants will find their way to the country. The proposition of federal distribution of immigrants is merely a clever illusion kept up to lead Congress astray from the restriction of immigration.

Higher Standards of Immigration.—As for the inferior, defective, and undesirable classes of immigrants, there is no protection except stringent selection. The Commissioner of Immigration at New York estimates that 200,000 of the million immigrants in 1903 were an injury instead of a benefit to the industries of the country, and he advocates a physical examination and the exclusion of those who fall below a certain physical standard. During the past ten years the educational, or rather, illiteracy test, has come to the front, and the advantages of this test are its simplicity and its specific application to those races whose standards are lowest.

Aliens awaiting Admission at Ellis Island

Much discussion has been carried on respecting this test, and there has been considerable misunderstanding and misrepresentation as to its probable effects. The principal mistake has been the assumption that it is designed to take the place of other tests of admission, and that therefore it would permit, for example, the most dangerous criminals—those who are intelligent—to enter this country. If we examine existing laws, and seek to understand the real nature of immigration restriction, we can see the character of this mistake. All of our legislation governing immigration should be described as *improvement* of immigration rather than *restriction* of immigration. The object has always been to raise the average character of those admitted by excluding those who fall below certain standards. And higher standards have been added from time to time as rapidly as the lawmakers perceived the need of bettering the quality of our future citizenship. Although in 1862 Congress had enacted a law prohibiting the shipment of Chinese coolies in American vessels, it was not until 1875 that the lawmakers first awoke to the evil of unrestricted immigration. In that year a law was enacted to exclude convicts and prostitutes. This law made an exception in favor of those who had been convicted of political offences. Next, in 1882, Congress added lunatics, idiots, paupers, and Chinese. In 1885 laborers under contract were for the first time to be excluded, but an exception was made in order to admit actors, artists, lecturers, singers, domestics, and skilled workmen for new industries. In 1891 the list of ineligibles was again extended so as to shut out not only convicts but persons convicted of crime, also "assisted" immigrants, polygamists, and persons with loathsome or dangerous contagious diseases. In 1903 the law added epileptics, persons who have had two or more attacks of insanity, professional beggars, and anarchists. Notwithstanding these successive additions of excluded classes, the number of immigrants has continually increased until it is greater to-day than in any preceding period, and while the standards have been raised in one direction, the average quality has been lowered in other directions. The educational and physical tests, while not needed for the races from Northwestern Europe, are now advocated as additions to the existing tests on account of the flood of races from Southeastern Europe.

The question of "poor physique" has come seriously to the front in recent reports of immigration officials. The decline in the average of physical make-up to which they call attention accompanies the increase in numbers of Southern and Eastern Europeans. While the commissioner at Ellis Island estimates that 200,000 immigrants are below the physical standards that should be required to entitle them to admission, the number certified by the surgeons is much less than this. Yet nine-tenths of even that smaller number are admitted, since the law excludes them only if other grounds of exclusion appear. That the physical test is practicable is shown by the following description of the qualities taken into account by the medical examiners at the immigrant stations; qualities which would be made even more definite if they were authorized to be acted upon:—

"A certificate of this nature implies that the alien concerned is afflicted with a body not only but illy adapted to the work necessary to earn his bread, but also but poorly able to withstand the onslaught of disease. It means that he is undersized, poorly developed, with feeble heart action, arteries below the standard size; that he is physically degenerate, and as such not only unlikely to become a desirable citizen, but also very likely to transmit his undesirable qualities to his offspring should he, unfortunately for the country in which he is domiciled, have any.

"Of all causes for rejection, outside of those for dangerous, contagious, or loathsome diseases, or for mental disease, that of 'poor physique' should receive the most weight, for in admitting such aliens not only do we increase the number of public charges by their inability to gain their bread through their physical inaptitude and their low resistance to disease, but we admit likewise progenitors to this country whose offspring will reproduce, often in an exaggerated degree, the physical degeneracy of their parents."

The history of the illiteracy test in Congress is a curious comment on lobbying. First introduced in 1895, it passed the House by a vote of 195 to 26, and the Senate in another form by a vote of 52 to 10. Referred to a conference committee, an identical bill again passed both Houses by reduced majorities. But irrelevant amendments had been tacked on and the President vetoed it. The House passed it over his veto by 193 to 37, but it was too late in the session to reach a vote in the Senate. Introduced again in 1898, it passed the Senate by 45 to 28, but pressure of the Spanish War prevented a vote in the House. The bill came up in subsequent Congresses but did not reach a vote. The lobby is directed by the steamship companies, supported by railway companies, the Hawaiian Sugar

Planters' Association, and other great employers of labor. By misrepresentation, these interested agencies have been able at times to arouse the fears of the older races of immigrants not affected by the measure. Their fears were groundless, for the illiteracy test is not a test of the English language, but a test of any language, and it applies only to those who are 15 years of age and over, but does not apply to wife, children, parents, or grandparents of those who are admitted. With these reasonable limitations it would exclude only 1 in 200 of the Scandinavians, 1 in 100 of the English, Scotch, and Finns, 2 or 3 in 100 of the Germans, Irish, Welsh, and French; but it would exclude one-half of the South Italians, one-seventh of the North Italians, one-third to two-fifths of the several Slav races, one-seventh of the Russian Jews, altogether one-fifth or one-fourth of the total immigration. But these proportions would not long continue. Elementary education is making progress in Eastern and Southern Europe, and a test of this kind would stimulate it still more among the peasants. Restrictive at first, it is only selective; it would not permanently reduce the number of immigrants, but would raise their level of intelligence and their ability to take care of themselves.

The foregoing principles do not apply to Chinese immigration. There the law is strictly one of exclusion and not selection. This distinction is often overlooked in the discussion of the subject. Respecting European, Japanese, and Korean immigration, the law *admits* all except certain classes definitely described, such as paupers, criminals, and so on. Respecting Chinese immigration the law *excludes* all except certain classes described, such as teachers, merchants, travellers, and students. In the case of European immigration the burden of proof is upon the immigration authorities to show that the immigrant should be excluded. In the case of the Chinese, the burden of proof is on the immigrant to show that he should be admitted. In the administration of the law the difference is fundamental. If the Chinese law is liberalized so as to admit doctors, lawyers, and other professional classes, against whom there is no objection, it can be done in one of two ways. It can name and specify the additional classes to be admitted. To this there is little objection, for it retains the existing spirit of the law. Or it can be reversed, and can admit all classes of Chinese except coolies, laborers, and the classes now excluded by other laws. If this were done, the enforcement of the law would break down, for the burden of proof would be lifted from the immigrant and placed on the examining board. The law is with great difficulty enforced as it is, but the evasions bear no comparison in number with those practised under the other law. European immigration is encouraged, provided it passes a minimum standard. Chinese immigration is prohibited unless it exceeds a maximum standard. One is selection, the other is exclusion. One should be amended by describing new classes *not* to be admitted, the other by describing classes which *may* be admitted.

This difference between the two laws may be seen in the effects of the restrictions which have from time to time been added to the immigration laws. Each additional ground of restriction or selection has not decreased the total amount of immigration, nor has it increased the proportion of those debarred from admission. In 1898, 3200 aliens were sent back, and this was 1.4 per cent of those who arrived. In 1901, 3900 were sent back, but this was only three-fourths of 1 per cent of those arriving. In 1906, 13,000 sent back were 1.2 per cent of the arrivals. Intending immigrants as well as steamship companies learn the standards of exclusion and the methods of evasion, so that the proportion who take their chances and fail in the attempt is very small. Nevertheless, this deportation of immigrants, though averaging less than 1 per cent, is a hardship that should be avoided. It has often been proposed that this should be done through examination abroad by American consuls or by agents of the Immigration Bureau. Attractive and humane as this proposal appears, the foreign examination could not be made final. It would remove the examiners from effective control, and would require a large additional force as well as the existing establishment to deport those who might evade the foreign inspection. It does not strike at the root of the evil, which is the business energy of the steamship companies in soliciting immigration, and their business caution in requiring doubtful immigrants to give bonds in advance to cover the cost of carrying them back. It is not the exclusion law that causes hardship, but the steamship companies that connive at evasions of the law. The law of 1903 for the first time adopted the correct principle to meet this evasion, but with a limited application. Since 1898, the Bureau had debarred increasing numbers on account of loathsome and contagious diseases. But these had already done the injury which their deportation was designed to prevent. In the crowded steerage the entire shipload was exposed to this contagion. Congress then enacted the law of 1903, not only requiring the steamship companies to carry them back, as before, but requiring the companies to pay a fine of $100 for every alien debarred on that account. In 1906, the companies paid fines of $24,300 on 243 such deportations. The principle should be extended to all classes excluded by law, and the fine should be raised to $500. Then every agent of the steamship companies in the remotest hamlets of Europe would be an immigration inspector. Their surgeons and officials already know the law and its standards of administration as thoroughly as the immigration officials. It only needs an adequate motive to make them cooperators with the Bureau instead of evaders of the law. Already the law of 1903 has partly had that effect. One steamship company has arranged with the Bureau to locate medical officers at its foreign ports of embarkation. However, the penalty is not yet heavy enough, and the Commissioner-General recommends its increase to $500. By extending the law to all grounds of deportation in addition to contagious diseases, the true source of hardship to debarred aliens will be dried up.